W9-BYA-865

Praise for Barbara McLennan
and *The Wealth of Jamestown*

"Everyone loves a great read. And this is a great read! It's got
everything a reader craves: intrigue, suspense, power struggles
of the mighty and the commoner, and the tantalizing clashes of
love and money. It's the inside story not taught in the schools
— one of the most tumultuous and exciting periods in history.
Louis XIV is on the throne of France, England has just fired
a king and hired William and Mary as new monarchs, and
Virginia simply wants to sell its tobacco, while pirates threaten
commerce on the seas. And the reader is on the inside of the
entire theatre of action on both sides of the Atlantic!"

DR. RICHARD OLIVER, bestselling author and
founder and CEO of American Sentinel University

"It is a privilege for Jamestown Settlement to have been part of
the inspiration for Barbara McLennan's latest work.
Through her fictional account, a period of Virginia's history is
vibrantly retold."

PHILIP G. EMERSON, Executive Director
Jamestown-Yorktown Foundation

The Wealth of Jamestown

by Barbara N. McLennan

© Copyright 2013 by Barbara N. McLennan

ISBN 978-1-938467-61-5

All rights reserved. No part of this publication may be reproduced, stored in a retrieval system, or transmitted in any form or by any means – electronic, mechanical, photocopy, recording, or any other – except for brief quotations in printed reviews, without the prior written permission of the author.

This is a work of fiction. All the characters in this book are fictitious, or are used fictitiously, and any resemblance to actual persons, living or dead, is purely coincidental. The names, incidents, dialogue, and opinions expressed are products of the author's imagination and are not to be construed as real.

Published by

an imprint of Morgan James Publishing

210 60th Street
Virginia Beach, Virginia, 23451
212-574-7939
www.koehlerbooks.com

Publisher
John Köehler

Executive Editor
Joe Coccaro

*Cover illustration by Keith Rocco,
provided by the National Park Service.*

DEDICATION

This book is dedicated to the memory of Professor Angus Maddison, who, in his career, made sense of economic and demographic history. Angus would have understood where Virginia's wealth came from and would likely have been able to figure out Virginia's rate of economic growth over the ninety years of Jamestown's existence.

Author's Note

This is a fictional story set during the lifetimes of the grandparents of many of America's Founding Fathers. It relies on names of persons and dates of events occurring in Jamestown, Virginia in the period 1685-1700. The story involves real people who lived in those times. Major historical events occurred as described: wars, marriages, deaths of kings and queens, arrivals and trials of governors. The behavior of the people affected by these events is purely fiction.

A representative assembly formed to debate legislation separate from an executive officer was well-established by 1685. There was widespread distrust of governors and clergymen sent from England to rule the colonies, a central theme of this novel.

The actions of certain historical characters throughout the novel can be corroborated. Edmund Andros and Francis Nicholson served as Governor and Lieutenant Governor during the period, and James Blair resurrected a college charter in 1693. Buildings were erected and burned down as described, and Blair presented complaints against Andros to an ecclesiastical court in London. Relatively few public documents survive, as Jamestown's state house burned several times.

THE WEALTH OF JAMESTOWN

A NOVEL OF COLONIAL VIRGINIA

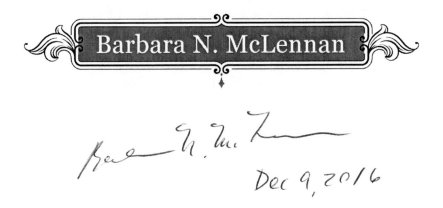

Barbara N. McLennan

Barb N. McLennan

Dec 9, 2016

VIRGINIA BEACH
CAPE CHARLES

CHAPTER 1

The small sloop was just at the horizon. The sun caught its main sail, and, though there was a stiff breeze, it seemed to be moving very slowly. The sailors on board were shouting, and local farmers and fishermen, hearing the noise, gathered on the shore of the York River near the main pier. William Roscoe heard cannon fire and saw puffs of smoke. An English warship had spotted the privateer and corralled it into the small port.

William knew the men on the private boat. The owner had a license from the Crown to conduct commercial shipping, but nobody on shore knew why the English were in pursuit. Had they attacked and captured goods from some other vessel? Did they have goods on board that the English wanted to tax or confiscate?

William was English and a sheriff appointed by the Governor, a representative of the King. But he was a Virginian, too. Like

his neighbors, his family's livelihood—in fact, their survival—
depended on tobacco. They needed their brave neighbors who
ran commercial ships to keep up a brisk business; when tobacco
prices were down, the privateers brought goods to Virginia that
people could use and sell. Everyone in Virginia appreciated the
risks these sailors and fishermen took. They were the lifeline to
the outside world— the only real means of trade in 1687.

As sheriff, William expected the captain of the warship to
demand that William take the privateer into custody, to have the
vessel inspected by customs agents, and to jail the privateer's
crew. The crew members were William's friends and neighbors.
The English warship captain was a stranger, someone he'd likely
never see again once the English ship set sail. The captain would
demand some kind of payment, maybe directly from William
formally, or, more likely, informally. The English always
expected to be paid for their services by Virginians.

William fidgeted and paced with anger. Nobody starved on
the English ship; the captain and crew plundered and vandalized
every port they visited. A young sheriff like William would have
to be careful dealing with the drunken sailors once they were
on shore. Virginia had few public buildings and very small jails,
and a shipload of drunken sailors was more than he cared to
confront.

William had talked this over with Sarah. They were engaged
to marry and she was concerned for his safety. Sarah had told
him that he shouldn't be alone in greeting any English military
unit, much less an English warship. He'd taken her advice and
had a small contingent of five militia men with him, armed with
muskets. They were three farmers and two fishermen, but had
come dressed for the occasion, each carrying his musket. They

all wore fine brown musketeer hats, with one side flat so they could carry their muskets on their shoulders. Though in different colors, they wore their best long wool coats and stockings, waist belts, bullet bags, and powder horns.

All this was small comfort. One shot from the warship could blow away the entire dock, with William and the five militia men standing on it.

William knew he had to project confidence and authority. He had to face a warship, and demand that its captain respect the law William represented. After all, this was Virginia, part of England. The captain, in Virginia waters, had to abide by the laws of the colony, ruled by a governor sent here by the King. William represented the King's peace, not the warship captain.

William was only twenty-two and just learning to make public announcements. He was much younger and more inexperienced than the English captain and, for that matter, most of the English crew. Compared to his neighbors and militia comrades, William was the youngest, but also the tallest, strongest and most fearless. He carried himself with a confidence well beyond his years. His willingness to serve had gained him the support of the local planters who'd recommended him to the Governor for appointment as sheriff; most farmers and planters weren't willing to leave their plantations during the growing season, but William had an interest in serving the public.

William contemplated a run for a seat in the House of Burgesses. He knew his neighbors personally, but they could hardly help him in times of trouble. If he became a burgess, he'd represent his county to the other burgesses, have a say in how the Governor raised money and could request military support when necessary.

Sarah wanted him to run for the House, as it would bring him to Jamestown where he would meet with Sarah's friends and family on a regular basis. William loved Sarah dearly, and respected her business acumen. She was a great advisor, knew the ins and outs of trade and commerce and had encouraged her fiancé to buy a ship using her dowry after they were married.

William thought hard about what to do about the English captain and crew and the demands they would make. He decided he would oblige the captain by taking the privateer into custody, but he wouldn't allow the English warship to dock. He'd find a way to get the privateer legally inspected for customs, and he'd direct the captain to go to Jamestown, which had better dock facilities, and where the Governor resided.

William stood on a wood barrel and announced his decision. As expected, his neighbors voiced their support for him. "Well done, William," several shouted. The militia members raised their muskets and marched in line to the small Yorktown dock.

William looked to the horizon and both ships were closing in on the shore. He thought, *How beautiful they are. What strength and grace they show. What a shame they had to come to shore in this small place—a small wooden pier on the edge of a great wood inhabited by the Pamunkey Indians.*

William worried that the sound of musket fire would anger the local Indians, and that he'd have trouble explaining the problems to the queen who ruled the tribe. He liked the queen, whom he knew quite well. A number of Virginians had married children and grandchildren of Pocahontas and Powhatan, and Virginia had enjoyed peace with them for nearly fifty years.

William feared that Virginia's peaceful coexistence with the natives and the calm of its agricultural settlements would soon be compromised. He knew that the English warship was at sea because of recent and impending wars in Europe, and likely because the English wanted to hamper Dutch shipping even though the recent peace treaty with Holland allowed Dutch ships to sail up the James. William thought, *We have enough problems without the French and the Dutch and the English.* He'd forgotten in that thought that he was English too.

⸙

William watched the warship chase the privateer into the small pier, and bear down on it. The large ship's cannon aimed at the small ship, ready to blow it out of the water. A ship's cannon shot could shatter not only the privateer, but also the dock and all the people assembled on it.

The English captain stood high on the starboard side of the ship facing the shore. He wore a splendid dress coat and appeared gigantic to the people looking at him from the land. His dark green jacket was embellished with gold brocade and he wore many medals. William knew that every captain looked different, as the English navy required no special uniform. This captain was wealthy, pompous and showy. The captain shouted, "Everyone, get back! This is a Royal Navy operation. We have a customs runner in custody."

William shouted from his standing position, "I am the sheriff, and there are no facilities on this river for you. You must go to Jamestown, where there is a proper dock. The Governor, our Chief Lord of the Admiralty, can see to your concerns."

"Then stand back, while I blow the criminals away!"

The crew on board the warship could be seen scurrying to load one of the great ship's cannons. They faced it out to the river, away from the shore and the private boat. While doing this, the warship crew shouted and joked with the people on shore. "Wait till you hear this, you bumpkins! Hold your ears!" The captain ordered the cannon fired and its thunder could be heard for miles. Every bird and frog seemed to scream and take flight all at once. But it was only a warning shot, and the captain was having fun with the locals.

William stood his ground. He wasn't going to be intimidated, and now he drew his sword and waved it in the air. He was furious and shouted, "You haven't proven the ship has broken any laws. That charge has to be presented before a court. This is Virginia and we enforce the King's laws here. If you act without legal justification, you are the criminal."

"But what will happen to the privateer, if we leave her here and go on to Jamestown? All of its cargo must be properly inspected by a customs agent and a full report made. We have reason to believe there are stolen goods on board."

"Mr. Harris here is a customs agent," said William, pointing to one of his five militia men. "We will prepare a proper report and take it to the Governor's offices in Jamestown. The ship will be kept here until we complete our review of what's on board. If something's amiss, we will keep the ship in custody."

William could see several Indians emerging from the woods behind the dock. Now he'd have to find a way to assure them of their safety, and the sight of the great ship surely frightened them.

The captain looked down on the small crowd of farmers, fishermen, Indians and militia men. He'd just completed a long voyage and his men were anxious for some shore leave. He could see only two small wooden buildings, both meant for storage and maintenance of the pier. There was no town, village, or tavern, and he wasn't sure his men would know how to deal with the Indians.

He shouted, "And what will you pay to have us abide with your foolish wishes?"

The warship crew laughed and guffawed. Some made faces at the crowd. The Indians began arming their bows, as several more appeared from the woods.

"You should take that up with the Governor. He is also Chief Lord of the Treasury, as well as the Lord Chief Justice. We understand he's interested in proper and fair enforcement of the laws." William was still furious and spoke in short clipped tones.

"Very well. We'll go on to Jamestown and pay our respects to the Governor. I am Captain Cavendish. Who shall I say is the sheriff?"

"I am William Roscoe, Sheriff of Warwick and Yorktown."

As the warship prepared to turn around, William turned to his friend George Harris, who knew nothing at all about customs declarations. "Who do you know that's seen a customs report?"

George was a fisherman who could read, but did very little writing. "Perhaps your intended, Miss Sarah? The Harrisons do a great deal of tobacco trading with Holland and Scotland. Perhaps she knows what appears on a customs report."

William saw the Indians take down their weapons. He greeted them and said "Nothing will happen here. They go on to Jamestown to see the Governor. Please tell the queen that we are all upset at the noise and commotion. I hope she is well and will not worry too much."

Two Indians acquainted with William responded. "What kind of people fire first and talk later? That shot surely frightened the deer, the turkeys, and anything else that moves."

"They're sailors who've been at sea too long. I apologize for them. At least they didn't fire at the shore."

CHAPTER 2

Sarah Harrison, daughter of Benjamin Harrison II, sat under a giant cypress tree near the deep blue James River. Fish were jumping out of the water and great eagles and ospreys soared above her. She was seventeen, tall with dark auburn hair, and flush with the full blossom of youth. She looked at William with sadness.

William had just ridden his horse over to the Harrison plantation. He was obviously very excited, anxious to tell her something. Thin, with light sandy-colored hair, he was imposing in his new clothes. He'd only recently been appointed sheriff, and had outfitted himself with a new red tunic to show his position.

Sarah complimented him. "How handsome you look! If I were a bandit of Warwick I'd surely not want to meet the wearer of such imposing clothes. You're ready for the House of Burgesses in such an outfit!"

William took a moment to exhale his anxiety and inhale his

fiancée's beauty. "I'm pleased you like it. Of course my clothes are nothing, when I see how lovely you look on this beautiful day."

William wasted little time after the pleasantries to vent his worries, which Sarah could read on his brow. "The Governor, Lord Effingham, has proposed new taxes, and people fear there may be riots. If we have peace for a while, I hope to stand for the seat. I believe I can represent our people."

Sarah laughed. "The riots will be in the House of Burgesses, not in the counties. If you wait to run, you can probably avoid meeting the rioters. I'm sure you have nothing to fear from the local planters. Father isn't worried about taxes, but about business. Tobacco trade is down and he blames the fear of new wars in Europe. Father has no patience for anything that might harm business."

William smiled. "You are his best business advisor, I'm sure. I suppose everyone fears poor trade, and some people fear starvation returning. Warships are patrolling our waters now. For what reason, no one can guess.

"Sarah, Have you ever seen a customs report? Could you prepare one for me? I've taken a ship into custody and need to prepare a report for the Governor."

She smiled coyly, clearly flattered by William's confidence in her. "I've seen many such documents. I'd be happy to make one up for you, but I need to know some particulars—the name of the ship, where it sailed, what's in its cargo. Has it been inspected?"

William then related his morning adventure. Sarah giggled. "What a man you are, to face down a warship with cannons firing! Take me to the packet today, and I'll make up the customs document. George can sign it, as Temporary Customs Inspector.

You're the sheriff and can make the appointment! I'll prepare your document appointing him, and you can sign it and show the customs people in Jamestown."

Sarah then stopped for a moment and turned to William. Four weeks earlier, William and Sarah, with the permission of their parents, had agreed to become engaged to be married. He'd not been her first suitor, but he'd been the most ardent. He knew she favored him above all others.

Both families executed a marriage contract, legally signed and witnessed: *These are to certify all persons in ye World, that I, Sarah Harrison, Daughter of Mr. Benja. Harrison, do & am fully resolved & by these presents do oblige myself (& cordially promise) to Wm. Roscow never to marry or to contract with any Man (during his life) only himself, to confirm these presents, I the above said Sarah Harrison do call the Almighty God to witness & so help me God.*

William cherished the moment when Sarah signed the document.

Sarah looked at William, and said, "William, you know that I've pledged to marry you and have said that I'd never marry another."

"I know that," said William. "My parents are delighted that you feel this way. I count the days when we'll live together as man and wife."

"This will never happen, William." Sarah was weeping.

William became red in the face. "How can this be? Just a few weeks ago your father was delighted with our engagement!" William took a few steps toward the river, but soon returned to Sarah who still sat under the great cypress tree.

"Answer me, Sarah, did you agree to this?"

Sarah trembled and mumbled, "My father has befriended Mr. James Blair, who's to become the Commissary of the Church of England. They sit together on the Governor's Council. Father believes that Blair will be a powerful man to know. Blair knows high-ranking people in London. He knows people on the Board of Trade. Blair also has contacts with factors in Scotland who import tobacco, and has promised father a good price on his tobacco crop."

"Why should that matter to us?" asked William. He knew Blair was a Scotsman, and thought it strange that Mr. Benjamin Harrison would befriend him. The Scotsmen in Virginia were either failed clergy who couldn't support themselves in England or Scotland, or small shopkeepers. Scotsmen were generally held in low esteem by Virginia planters, who thought of them as money-hungry or useless drunkards.

William shouted, "Does your father put business with Scotland ahead of his daughter's happiness?"

Sarah now wept openly. "Father has promised me to Blair as a wife and insists that I break the contract with you. He'll pay you fifty pounds[1*] for the trouble."

"Do you agree to this?"

"I have no choice; my father insists."

"What do you think of James Blair?"

"He's already an old man. Some say he's already thirty, and he looks forty—closer to my father's age than mine. He also has that sallow London look of a man who never sees the daylight. He speaks in a high pitch Scottish whine, and forever wears black. He's not dashing like you, William. He has no future. He'll always be a grim, dark churchman."

---

1   *Approximately $100,000 in 2009 money.

"Oh my poor dear, what shall we do?"

"You can do nothing. You're a sheriff and soon will be a burgess. I can't oppose my father."

They embraced, but now both wept. After a bit, William spoke. "I wanted our marriage and will always remember you. I hope you can find some happiness. I know that I likely never will."

Sarah replied, sobbing softly. "I said I would never marry another, and I meant it. Blair will never own me. You are free to find another. And I will help you with the customs report."

They both mounted their horses and went back to the York and the packet ship.

<hr/>

When Sarah and William arrived at the privateer docked on the York, they saw the captain of the ship, four crew members and several passengers. The passengers were two middle-aged couples and four teenage children. They were sitting on various boxes and barrels unloaded from the ship. They congregated in the shade of a small wooden maintenance shed at the end of the pier.

Some traveling bags and trunks had been unloaded, as well as two barrels of rum. The captain spoke to a well-dressed older lady who had arrived in a wagon, accompanied by two well-armed young men. The crew looked at the barrels, but had obviously been restrained by the captain and the lady.

The day was warm and sunny, and a light breeze blew from the deep blue river. Light waves brushed the shore while birds sung happily and tree frogs croaked rhythmically. The passengers looked tired but happy to be on land, and their conversation was muffled but apparently good-humored. Sarah and William could hear the sound of speech but couldn't understand what was being said.

Sarah and William dismounted and tied their horses to a post along the side of the shed. As they approached the people, Sarah said to William, "I've met the lady. She is Mrs. John Custis. She's been widowed several times and retains an interest in business. My father has used her ships to bring cargo to Europe. She's probably here because she owns the sloop."

William approached the people and noticed that the passengers' conversation wasn't in English. He introduced himself to the lady, saying "Greetings to all from Jamestown and Yorktown. I am the sheriff, William Roscoe, and I've promised Captain Cavendish a full customs report. I hope all are safe from your long journey."

The lady introduced herself. "Hello, sheriff. My name is Mrs. Tabitha Scarborough Smart Brown Custis, and I own the *Pretty Polly* here. Thank you for taking the time to visit. I understand you had an interesting meeting with Captain Cavendish."

The crew guffawed and the captain laughed. "You should have seen Willie standing on top of that barrel! He never moved an inch, though the cannon could have blown away just about everything else. I thought the Indians would let some arrows fly, though that wouldn't have done much. Good old Willie just invoked the law. We were surprised to get off so easily."

Mrs. Custis said to William, "Well, we are in your debt. These people are cousins to Mr. Smart, my first husband. They are French and have escaped the wrath of their king, who's made their religion impossible in France. They are Protestants, Huguenots, and don't accept the Church of Rome."

William thought about this and looked at Sarah. They were both mystified about this attention to religion that still held sway in Europe. William didn't know what to say, so Sarah introduced herself. "Let me add my welcome to all to our colony. I've accompanied William to help him prepare the customs forms. My name is Sarah Harrison and my father owns a tobacco plantation over at Surry. I believe we've met at my home, Mrs. Custis."

Mrs. Custis and the passengers now stood, all looking at Sarah and William. At first Mrs. Custis raised her eyebrows, but soon broke out in a friendly smile. She spoke to Sarah, "Yes. Thank you for helping us. I understand you'll soon be wed. I wish you happiness and good fortune. Mr. Custis and I will be attending your wedding." Then, looking at William, in a warm Virginia drawl, she smiled again and said "It's an honor to meet you, sheriff. I welcome your and Miss Harrison's assistance, as I wasn't aware of any customs agents in these parts. I didn't quite know how to handle the legal matters."

William explained the plan, that he would appoint George Harris as Temporary Customs Inspector, that Sarah would prepare a written form, and that he would carry the document to Jamestown where the Governor sat. He expected to have to deal somehow with Captain Cavendish once he got to Jamestown.

Mrs. Custis turned to the passengers speaking in French, and the teenagers took notice. Apparently none spoke English. They appeared to be relieved, and one of the older men took out a small leather pocket book, which Mrs. Custis told him to put away.

She then turned to Sarah and William. "My guests feel indebted to you, but I've told them that I would take care of any charges. Have you thought about charges, Mr. Roscoe?"

William again didn't know what to say, so Sarah interceded again. "We thank you for whatever you think is appropriate. I'm sure William will be grateful for anything that would earn him a proper income. He's thinking of running for the House of Burgesses, and will need assistance if he wins. He also may have to make some sort of payment to Cavendish when he gets to Jamestown. The English have a way of demanding payment for whatever they do."

Mrs. Custis laughed. "Yes, that's to be expected. They think money grows on Virginia's trees, and they're not shy about asking, especially if they have bought themselves fancy uniforms and shoot off cannons. You know, my father was Speaker of the House back in the old days before Cromwell sent his army over. As I recall, Cromwell's men went into Maryland and murdered a few priests. Catholics from Maryland ran away to Virginia, and stayed until the King was restored. Strange, isn't it? Now the Protestants are running away to Virginia. What do you think of that, William?"

William knew as much history as any Virginian, which was basically what his parents had told him and what he could remember himself. He said, "I believe in the law. Ordinary people have to feel safe in their livelihoods or the colony will die. We welcome everyone who wants to build the colony. If they're not Church of England, they must pay the tax and not molest other people. We certainly don't oppose them coming to live here if they have trades and skills to offer."

"Well said, William. You know in Massachusetts, where my father lived early in his life, they murder Quakers. They particularly love executing witches. My French relations, though they are Protestant, didn't feel safe going there. Let me introduce you. They are Mr. and Mrs. Bardon, their son Pierre and daughter Suzanne; and Mr. and Mrs. Du Bois, and their son Henri and daughter Diane." The French people rose and smiled at William.

Mrs. Du Bois said something to Mrs. Custis, who laughed and said to William, "My cousin admires your fine red tunic. She offers to make you a new one, perhaps in another color. The whole family is skilled in making clothes. I'm sure we'll find a place for them in Middle Plantation or Charles Towne. The Bardons are traders and, like my father, own ships. We must talk about business sometime, William. And when there is an election, you must come and see me. My brother Charles knows most of the members. I'll be happy to help you."

The captain and Sarah then conversed about the customs declarations. They agreed that two barrels of rum would be declared and customs duties paid. They would make no mention of French passengers. Sarah would prepare the document and leave it for William, who would get the necessary signatures and collect the customs duties from Mrs. Custis.

But Mrs. Custis had come prepared. She tossed a packet of tobacco notes to William, saying "This should cover any customs duties or other charges William. If it's insufficient, you should probably arrest somebody. If there is some left over, keep it for yourself. You've been very brave."

CHAPTER 3

James Blair came to Virginia in 1685. On the eve of his marriage to Sarah Harrison, the Scotsman was pleased with himself. He'd accomplished what he was told to do by superiors, and now he'd be rewarded with the position of Commissary of the Church of England in Virginia and take a full seat on the Governor's Council. Blair would collect three salaries, one for each of his titles: parish minister, Church Commissary, and Governor's Council member. It hadn't been easy. He felt secure now, but he'd been through many trials before he got to this point.

For his day, James Blair was an educated man. A son of an Anglican preacher, brother to another, with a younger brother who was a doctor, he felt he had to prove something to his family. He'd always been the runt of the Blair litter. Of slight build, with light mousy brown hair that hung straight to his shoulders, he had a pale pinkish complexion. He had a high pitched voice that carried across a room, but was small and girlish. He hated feeling that people looked down on him, and now that he was in Virginia, he aimed to change that.

He recalled his first ministry. In 1679, after six years of study at Edinburgh, he passed his examinations, received the degree of Master of Arts, and was ordained a minister of the Church of Scotland. He received a ministry in Cranston, a thinly populated rural parish not far from Edinburgh that held a twelfth-century church.

From the beginning, Blair got off on the wrong foot with his new parishioners. The area was poor and rural, and the minister's residence was a small stone cottage with a leaky roof. Of course, many of the farmers in the area lived in very similar small dwellings, suffered hard lives and had little to spare. But they were grateful when the church sent them a minister.

Blair quickly contracted with two men to repair the roof and purchased a bed, a chair and a writing table. He also hired a housekeeper to prepare his meals. He expected the parish to pay for these expenses.

Of course, his bed and writing desk, as well as his silver pen, were purchased in Edinburgh near the university. The parishioners of Cranston had never seen such fine stuff. They refused to pay for them, and Blair owed Edinburgh merchants, with little prospect of finding the necessary funds to pay them. He was in trouble and he knew it.

Blair talked to his acquaintances at the university, and one of his former professors, Rev. Lawrence Charteris, invited him to dinner. Charteris said to James, "Have you had any thoughts of politics?"

"Not really, sir. I've been trying to make ends meet in

Cranston, and my bumpkins refuse to pay for my pen, paper and writing desk. How am I supposed to prepare a sermon for people like this?"

"You should remind them of their duties to church and God, and you as their minister."

"That's fine to say. Farmers listen with one ear and do what they see fit after the sermon's over."

"Perhaps you've been a little extravagant for the farmers of Cranston. Maybe you should perform a few marriages, see to a few funerals, and then ask again. Make friends with the people, James: they are your real livelihood. When you go to a rural area you will always be one of many expenses to the people living there."

"I'm afraid my training in Edinburgh has left me ill-suited for a parish of uneducated farmers. Cranston has hardly any tradesmen; most of the people who read belong to John Knox's Presbyteries."

"Well, that brings us to politics, doesn't it? Scotland is nearly in religious rebellion. People here won't abide a Catholic king, and you know that King James has become Catholic and has asked all ministers to swear allegiance to him in a formal oath. That would make ministers of the Church of England and Church of Scotland swear to uphold a Catholic. What do you think of that?"

Blair had never really thought of high politics or the whims of kings and aristocrats. He'd only considered himself and the possibilities of increasing his personal status and income. He said, "What alternative do we have? We can hardly join the Presbyteries."

"I plan to resign my professorship here in Scotland and go

to London. We have some Edinburgh people in the Church of England who'll find a place for those who won't subscribe to a test oath."

"Well, perhaps there's a way for me out of Scotland as well. I'll think about it carefully."

Blair didn't think long. Bill collectors had already started knocking at his door. After hearing that Charteris had refused to sign the test oath and resigned his professorship, Blair followed suit and resigned his meager ministry.

Blair went to London, where he visited Gilbert Burnet, a well-placed Scottish minister who knew Professor Charteris. Burnet found employment in London for the disestablished clergy who'd been Charteris's students.

For Blair, Burnet found a position as a law clerk in the Rolls Office, where Burnet held the position of preacher. The Master of the Rolls was a senior judge of civil lawsuits in England, and in this post, Blair learned the ins and outs of the London legal system and met the leading lawyers of the day, as well as Henry Compton, the bishop of London.

Aggressive, ambitious and articulate, Blair learned to handle friends and foes. He did favors for superiors, and spoke negatively about competitors. He was a talented lobbyist and helped people who paid him for his efforts. His personal life was a mystery to everyone, but he had no strong attachments to anyone other than his father and brothers. Blair never had a romantic relationship that anyone knew about. He feared the company of women and much preferred young boys.

In 1684 Burnet preached a sermon on Guy Fawkes Day attacking popery. The King, as a Catholic, interpreted this as an attack on the monarchy itself, and Burnet was removed from his post. Blair, without Burnet's support, was in danger of losing his position. He went to see Henry Compton.

Blair had already achieved a reputation. Compton knew that Blair had few friends, but was ambitious. Other church officials in Lambeth Palace, the seat of the Anglican Church in London, disliked and resented him. He'd accepted payments for legal favors, and some of his clients were very unpopular at Lambeth.

Compton received Blair is his private quarters. "These are difficult days for the church, James. How goes it with you?"

"As you know, Reverend Burnet has been removed from his post at the Rolls. I fear all of us Anglicans will be in trouble with our Catholic king."

"Burnet is a fine fellow, well-liked by many. He'll find something to his liking, I'm sure."

"But I fear that I will be out on my ear before he sets himself in a decent place."

"How about another parish? You were in Cranston for only a short while. That was Scotland, not exactly a warm place for Anglican ministers."

"Well, I was hoping for a way to make a decent living."

"Here's a thought. How about a parish in Virginia? The colony is Anglican, and the tobacco crop keeps them well off. A vestry in Virginia will pay a decent living."

"Well, I hope you're not sending me away to get rid of me."

"James, you are well-educated and nearly thirty. You should by now have a family and be a leader in your community. Lobbying for miscreants coming into the Rolls office isn't what you were trained for. We have a few places available, and Virginia is a plum. It's our richest colony. Some of the planters there are very rich."

"But it's so far away, and life there is probably no better than Cranston."

"James, if you play your cards right, all will be well. You'll be a member of the Governor's Council, and meet the right people. If you find a proper wife and enter their society, I can promise you the post of Commissary of the Church of England. You'll receive a stipend for that, a stipend for serving on the Governor's Council, and a payment from your vestry. I suggest you take the Henrico vestry. Henrico includes some very large tobacco plantations."

Blair knew he had to take the offer, as the alternative was too frightening to contemplate. England and Europe had spent nearly a hundred years killing people over religious differences. At least Virginia was Anglican. Blair knew he had to become Commissary if anything was to work out for him.

Blair planned his approach to the Virginia gentry. Blair's younger brother, Archibald, was a medical doctor and approved the use of tobacco to many of his patients for medical purposes. Dr. Blair sold tobacco to his patients and knew the major Scottish importers. Blair talked to his brother about Virginia, and Archie was very supportive of the idea. "Virginia has the world's best tobacco. I know several factors who'd be delighted to help you export to Glasgow. You should go, James. You could become rich!"

***

Blair arrived in Virginia in 1685. He soon met Benjamin Harrison of Surry, a member of the Governor's Council, where Blair sat as the provisional Commissary of the Church of England. As a Council member, he developed the idea that it was right for him to govern others, though politics in London was quite different than in Virginia. Virginians may have been taxed and commanded by the King in London and his Board of Trade, but as far as the tobacco planters were concerned, the only thing that mattered was whether they could get their tobacco to market.

Blair found Virginians to be simple, or even simple-minded. When he met Benjamin Harrison at his first Governor's Council meeting, he learned that Harrison was a family man. In small talk he heard that Harrison was concerned for his fifteen year-old daughter, and was disappointed that she seemed uninterested in men of his choosing.

Blair immediately asked about business and Harrison replied, "We in Virginia try to survive and support our families. We grow the crops, but if Europe is at war, we will have difficulty delivering the tobacco. That's a threat to all our livelihoods. All of us have lost family members to starvation here, while Europe has war after war."

Blair responded, "Yes, kings are always after each other's properties. Our king and governor both are Catholic, so we must all fear a return to civil war over religion."

"Europe fights over religion, while we watch and pay for it. We are as Anglican as any colony, but we've never murdered people over that in Virginia. It's well remembered here how Cromwell's army in Maryland killed a few priests and that Catholics from Maryland ran to Virginia for protection. European wars cost us dearly. If we don't deliver tobacco, we can starve. We're never far from starvation here."

Blair replied, "I know many members of the Board of Trade quite well, especially the Whig members who oppose our Catholic king. Have you thought of sending tobacco to Scotland? I can get you a good price from factors there. If you ship a northern route, you may avoid the French and Spanish ships more easily."

Harrison found the proposition interesting. He and Blair talked a few times and developed a business relationship. After a year, Harrison delivered several tobacco shipments to factors in Glasgow. He was happy with the price he got in Scotland and looked forward to continuing his tobacco trade.

By 1687, Blair felt he was a friend of Benjamin Harrison II. He pressed for the hand in marriage of Harrison's daughter, Sarah. Though she had recently become engaged to a local boy, Harrison accepted Blair's proposal. In exchange for a substantial dowry that he'd give to his daughter, Benjamin Harrison would continue and expand contacts with tobacco factors in Scotland. Blair looked forward to his wedding, and becoming a power in Virginia.

<hr />

Sarah Harrison spoke to her mother, "Why must there be a legal wedding for father to gain a factor for our tobacco? Isn't the tobacco good enough? Can't we sell it to Holland? Why to Scotland?"

Sarah's mother, Hannah Harrison, knew Sarah loved William. But in Virginia, family had to come before personal preferences.

"You know that times are hard right now. William stood up to a battleship just last week. If Europe's wars come here, there will be no farms, no food for anyone, and nobody to protect us from who-knows-what-brutality. Thousands die in Europe every year because one king wants the lands of another. We have to sell our tobacco, and your father is seeing to all of our interests in allowing this marriage."

Sarah sat grim-faced and ready to cry, but there was no alternative. If her father, a member of the Governor's Council, felt he needed to protect his tobacco sales by a deal with a Scotsman, his daughter couldn't persuade him otherwise. Sarah admired and respected her father, but she hated feeling like just another one of his commodities.

"You'll be a lovely bride, and people from everywhere are looking forward to today," Hannah said. " You'll find that your father knows his business. Without it, we'd all starve. There soon will be war in Europe, you know. We must do whatever's necessary to make ends meet."

"Make ends meet? We could sell off half our land and still make ends meet! What good is selling me to a Scottish priest? He brings no land or wealth of his own."

"He knows important people in England. He knows people on the Board of Trade who govern all of Virginia's trade. Also, his brother is a doctor who imports tobacco into Scotland. Archie Blair knows all of the great Scottish factors and importers."

"So father would sell me for a Scottish factor? I'm sorry Captain Cox was so stupid that he couldn't talk. At least he had the appearance of a proper gentleman."

Captain Cox was in the Governor's militia. Sarah had agreed to marry him two years earlier. Then only fifteen, she met him when he came to the Harrison home for dinner. Sarah was overwhelmed by Cox's presence and grandeur, his stunning military uniform and his physical height. After the dinner Benjamin had talked to his daughter.

"Sarah, do you care for this man?"

"Oh, father. He is magnificent. I'd love a husband like him."

Harrison, heeding the teenager's emotions, said, "Very well, we'll arrange a wedding feast and invite the neighbors. But you should have a walk with the captain and get to know him a little better."

Harrison spoke with Cox and agreed to host a grand wedding entertainment. Sarah's dowry was agreed, and for the next few days Sarah and the Captain Cox took long walks together in the garden, wandered down to the river's edge, and rode horses through the woodlands. Through all of this, Sarah tried to talk to Cox, but received only single word answers and odd sound effects in return. It was if Cox didn't know how to hold a conversation with a woman. Sarah couldn't imagine spending a lifetime like this. She realized that Cox was more show than personality, and she wanted personality. She wanted to marry someone to whom she could talk.

The day before the scheduled wedding Sarah pleaded to her father. "Father, I can't marry this man. He's too pompous and above me. He thinks I'm a cow or a horse. He doesn't know how to hold a conversation. I want someone with more intelligence."

Benjamin Harrison was shocked, especially since he'd arranged a grand and sumptuous wedding. He decided to keep the wedding dinner, but there would be no wedding. He talked to Cox, whom he paid fifty pounds for his troubles.

⁕

Hannah remembered the occasion with some amusement and embarrassment. Her daughter could be stubborn and impetuous. Hannah feared that Sarah would, once again, get cold feet and rebuff the Scotsman, once again embarrassing the

Harrison family. She reminded Sarah that she was expected to behave properly in front of numerous invited guests.

"Now, don't be angry and forget about personal insults. Nobody will defend you if you behave badly," Hannah said "You'll be given a proper dowry and this is still Virginia. The property will be yours to keep or spend as you please. Keep a proper business head, and you'll be one of the wealthiest women this side of the Atlantic, even while other people fear starvation due to the war."

"Mother," Sarah was openly weeping, "I can't go through with this farce! Everyone knows I've been engaged to William. We pledged never to marry others. I meant that when I signed the contract in front of the clerk."

"Sarah, a marriage is a family decision made for what's best for the family. If you are wise and sensible, you can arrange your life to be happy and fulfilling without marriage to William. You must use your intelligence and plan for a future with the Commissary."

Sarah wept bitter tears. Her mother approached and held her briefly. Then Hannah said, "It's time for you to try the dress. You'll look lovely in this shade of green."

A few hours later, Sarah Harrison stood next to her bridegroom, James Blair, the Anglican minister sent to Virginia by the archbishop of London. They stood in the garden of the Harrison's Surry Plantation in a large space cleared and decorated for the wedding. Behind her, her father, Benjamin Harrison II, waited for the ceremony to conclude.

The month was June, 1687, and the garden burst with spring blossoms. Reverend Smith conducted the traditional service under flowering pear trees, witnessed by over three hundred guests. Almost the entire House of Burgesses and their families attended, as well as the Governor's Council. Representatives of the local Indian tribes came, and the chiefs were dressed splendidly. All of the guests wore their finest attire, but the garden swallowed the colors of the ladies fine silk gowns and men's ceremonial uniforms and waistcoats. Only Blair wore his black churchman's robe.

Reverend Smith spoke the vows. "Do you promise to love, honor and obey?" Sarah, still a vivacious girl of seventeen with a mind of her own, spoke up loudly. She wore her dark hair high upon her head, and with her high cheekbones and imposing posture towered over her impish groom. She wore a luscious spring green silk gown with a deep neckline that showed off her ample breasts.

Her piercing soprano voice could be heard by every guest. *"No obey!"* she affirmed. Reverend Smith looked at Blair who shrugged and said nothing. Smith repeated the vows again, and again Sarah spoke up clearly. *"No obey!"*

Reverend Smith tried a third time, and received the same response. Knowing that Blair was his superior and determined to marry into one of Virginia's finest families, Smith pronounced the couple man and wife. Smith had never had this experience before. The father of the bride said nothing.

The Bishop of London kept his promise and appointed Blair his Commissary of the Church of England and personal representative on the Virginia Governor's Council. Blair received a salary for this title.

Blair's income was growing,[2*] but he wasn't able to provide

---

2   ·In 1689, when he became Commissary, Blair received a total income of several hundred pounds, while Virginia planters lived on thousands. A hundred pounds in earnings in 1690 would be about $233,000 in 2009. The Governor's salary

his bride with a house and the comforts to which she was accustomed. Sarah controlled her own dowry, from which she purchased clothes and horses and servants, and sometimes new land and properties. She maintained an active interest in business and kept close ties with her father and brother.

Blair knew his status in Virginia was well below that of the average Virginia planter who sat in the Governor's Council or House of Burgesses. His status was well below that of his wife, and Virginia, strangely to Blair, allowed substantial property rights to women, whether widowed or married.

In 1690 Blair's brother Archie came to Virginia. Archie's wife had died and left him with a young son. Seeking to supplement his income as a doctor, Archie started a retail establishment near Bruton Parish Church in Middle Plantation, seven miles away from Jamestown. There he sold imported products from Europe, as well as foodstuffs and alcoholic beverages. James held a fifty percent interest in his brother's business and received payment from that enterprise.

James was in a fix. His opportunity for advancing his prestige and income were limited. Virginia suffered a steep fall in tobacco prices due to the war with France, which broke out when William of Orange became King of England in 1689. Small farmers were on the verge of starvation; large planters were amassing debts. The people feared Indian attacks and a possible French invasion, and they lived spread out among large distant plantations.

was two thousand pounds, or $4.6 million in today's dollars. See "Purchasing Power of British Pounds from 1264 to Present," *Measuring Worth*, www.measuringworth. com.

James couldn't understand Virginia's aversions to building towns and the amenities of city life. The colony had no great buildings, no imposing churches or public buildings. Courts were makeshift matters, meeting in public taverns or private homes. There were few streets and virtually no shops. Visitors had to impose on the hospitality of residents. The few hotel rooms were tiny places in the upper floors above taverns, and few taverns had upper floors. Simple craftsmen were few and far between. There were no libraries and few theaters, no public places in which to see and be seen, and no college. People were armed wherever they went, and to enter onto someone's property in the countryside, even by accident, was to invite murder. The law, such as it was, protected the property owner.

Virginians, however, were extraordinarily hospitable. They welcomed invited guests and properly introduced strangers into their homes, treating them royally. Rich people in Virginia were very rich. Their homes were graced with luxuries that outstripped the great houses of Europe. They hung gilded mirrors on the walls, lay extravagant Persian carpets atop their dining tables, and ate off the finest Dutch chinaware. Their clothes were of the finest English woolens and Chinese silks. For fashion, they turned to France, though styles were a year or two dated, as it took time for sewing patterns to cross the Atlantic.

Though they had no college or university, Virginians were well read. The system of home learning and studying religion from books and tutors had produced generations of people who could discuss philosophy, keep accounts, and perform scientific experiments. Virginians knew their history, and aggressively defended their decisions. They believed they were English, but James knew that the English did not share the Virginians' outlook on the world.

James Blair had seen the great aristocrats of England through his work in the office of the Master of the Rolls in London. He'd seen how lawyers lobbied for aristocrats and wheedled large sums of money from the king's treasury. None of the aristocrats he knew in London were nearly as wealthy or well read as many of the wealthy Virginia planters and their families.

James himself felt superior to others, by virtue of his formal education and his titles as Reverend and Commissary. He saw the world as a hierarchy, with the church and churchmen at the top. He expected Virginians to understand and accept his superiority, but Virginians didn't see the world as a neat bureaucracy, with people's statuses based on names or family connections. In Virginia, wealth had come to people who survived and worked hard for it, and many Virginians had died in the process. The death rate due to disease was still high, much higher than in England.

The wealthiest planters didn't lounge around a court house in fine silks. They went out to the country, oversaw the planting, selling and shipping of goods, and saw to the defense of their property and marriage of their daughters to properly wealthy grooms. Virginians had no aristocratic titles, and titles gained in Europe went nowhere in Virginia society; money and the ability to fight in the militia counted most.

In 1690, the year he became Commissary, James Blair convened a meeting of the two dozen Anglican preachers living in Virginia. He was their superior, appointed by London as Commissary. He proposed that four ecclesiastical courts be established to enforce ecclesiastical laws, and punish swearing, fornication and other violations of the Ten Commandments. At the meeting Blair issued a proclamation:

[The Lord Bishop of London]...has commanded the Ecclesiastical Jurisdiction to be impartially executed in order to a speedy Reformation of the lives of both Clergy and Laity within this Colony; and for this end has by a publick instrument under his hand and Episcopal Seal nominated and appointed me James Blair his Commissary within the Dominion and colony forsd, as the sd instrument bearing date the i5th day of Decr in the year of our Lord 1689 doth more largely contain and express:

Now know ye yt I the sd James Blair by virtue of the forsd Commission do in the name of the Right Revd Father in God Henry Lord Bishop of London and with the Advice of the Clergy of this Colony at their General Meeting forsd. Certify to all persons Concerned yt I intend to revive and put in execution the Ecclesiastical laws against all cursers. Swearers & blasphemers, all whoremongers, fornicators and Adulterers, all drunkards ranters and profaners of the Lords day and Contemners of the Sacraments, and agt all other Scandalous Persons, whether of the Clergy or Laity within this dominion and Colony of Virginia...

James Blair, the lobbyist, had forgotten to get to know the people whose support he needed. Virginia's ministers were an easygoing lot, used to riding circuit from parish to parish. Blair wished to appoint himself a chief judge of the clergy with Anglican ministers serving as his subordinates. He didn't offer them an increase in salary or security.

Preachers in Virginia were used to serving their parishes

and vestries, and saw no advantage in accepting a new overseer. They let it be known throughout the vestries that they opposed the new Commissary's proposal.

Blair visited the new acting Lieutenant Governor, Francis Nicholson. Nicholson had come to Virginia after serving as governor of New York. He was an experienced administrator, and well known for supporting church and education, often with his own money.

Blair began the conversation. "Welcome to Virginia. I understand that matters are not yet settled in London."

"Yes, Commissary. The new king is already at war with France. I'm afraid the Sun King wants a relative on every throne, and a Catholic to head every country. This may be a serious, long war. Virginia is already suffering from the decline in trade. How can I help you?"

"Well, you know we have very few ministers for the number of parishes. We have twenty, for fifty parishes. They can hardly be expected to enforce normal church teachings when riding from circuit to circuit as they do."

"What can I do to help?"

"I would like to establish some ecclesiastical courts that would enforce the normal church teachings. They could reach decisions on individuals—such as drunkards and fornicators— and hand the cases over to your sheriffs."

Nicholson thought about this. He was new and only a Lieutenant Governor. He hoped to be a full governor with full salary someday, and he knew that the key to Virginia was tobacco, and getting along with the House of Burgesses.

He asked Blair, "With whom have you discussed this? Have you brought it before the Governor's Council? Have you talked to anyone in the House of Burgesses?"

Blair responded, "This is a matter of church governance. It has nothing to do with the obligations of the Governor or the assembly."

"But then why do you come to see me? You want the sheriffs to do your bidding, and that will take their time from other matters. Where am I to get more sheriffs, if you produce many cases?"

Blair was surprised at Nicholson. He thought this would be an opportunity for a man who'd built many Anglican churches to support his commissary. "Don't you support an effort by the church to govern the parishes?" Blair asked quizzically.

"Of course I do," Nicholson huffed. " I've built many Anglican churches, all the way from Maine to the Jerseys. You'll not find a better Anglican than me."

Blair waited, a little agitated, as he didn't really understand what Nicholson was thinking. Nicholson then said, "Go ahead with your courts. I'll instruct the sheriffs to expect cases from them."

Nicholson then spent the next few weeks speaking to members of the House of Burgesses. Times were hard and the House simply couldn't find money to expand the offices of the sheriffs. Nicholson then ordered that no ecclesiastical court proceedings would be pursued. Blair's proposed church courts died in eight months.

CHAPTER 4

Daniel Parke had a clear view of himself in the world. He was the master of his household. If he had debts, that was his own choice. He would defend himself as he was raised to do, on horseback, with swords or pistols or muskets, or whatever weapon was at hand. If he took a woman to bed, that was also his choice. No woman would order him about, particularly a wife. Or, more specifically, a mother-in-law.

In 1691 Parke lived lavishly in Virginia, almost as lavishly as he'd lived the prior three years in England. In his late father's English home in Surry, he entertained, gambled and took a jolly mistress, a Mrs. Berry, who loved the gifts he gave her, the parties, the entry to aristocratic society.

Mr. Berry hadn't liked Parke at all, and issued a challenge when he learned that Mrs. Berry carried Parke's child. Parke was licentious, but no fool. He lived his life at the expense of his family, his plantation in Virginia, and his wife's family, who paid his debts. Parke would have enjoyed facing down Mr. Berry in a proper duel. But public opinion was different in England. Unlike Virginia, there actually were laws and customs that people respected. England was overrun with lawyers and moralists. He couldn't take the chance of being denounced from a pulpit or being dragged into court.

Parke was delighted when Mrs. Berry presented him with a son. He insisted on the boy being christened Julius Caesar Parke. He wanted the boy to grow up in his image, as a master, a leader, a warrior. For that reason he brought his son and mistress back to Virginia to live in his home with his wife, Jane, and his two legitimate daughters, Frances and Lucy.

Parke, though still in his twenties, saw himself as a leader of Virginia society. A member of the Virginia militia with some military training, he was a vestryman in the only church in Jamestown and held a seat in the House of Burgesses. He was a handsome, athletic man with fine features and high cheekbones. He was tall and rode his horse high in the saddle.

His wife, whom he'd married when they were teenagers, was an attentive mother and never complained of anything Parke did, no matter how outrageous. He had no head for business, and Jane Ludwell Parke did most of the work of running their plantation.

His mother-in law, Lady Frances Culpeper Stephens Berkeley Ludwell, was another story. Lady Frances had married three royal governors, and, many believed, still exercised considerable power and influence. She had inherited much property in Carolina from her first husband, governor of the Albemarle settlements. After he died, she married the Governor of Virginia. When her second husband died she inherited much

Virginia property, including the large governor's palace, Green Spring.

Lady Frances clearly knew the right people at the royal court in London, and managed to get her third husband, Philip Ludwell, Jane's father, appointed governor of Carolina. Lady Frances had no children of her own, but felt close to the Ludwell children, whom she'd raised from early childhood. She was especially close to Jane and Jane's children.

At an early afternoon dinner, while Jane was still at the table, Lady Frances said to Daniel, "What do you mean by bringing your bastard and his besotted mother into this house? How dare you belabor us with the debts of your license?"

Parke laughed, "Lady Frances, but you are English, are you not? All English gentlemen have their friends and wards. Why shouldn't I? At least Jane shall have the company of my boy, Julius Caesar."

Jane knew her husband's moods and usually resisted direct confrontation. This evening, she rose from the dinner table and walked to where she stood behind Lady Frances and looked her husband in the face.

Jane Ludwell wasn't beautiful, but she was tall, imposing and very intelligent. She was well respected in business dealings and Daniel didn't intimidate her. She knew the plantation's finances much better than Daniel. She knew how much his profligacy and gambling had cost her and the family. Over the last several years she'd had to sell off properties to make ends meet. It wasn't easy keeping a plantation going in times of war.

"Daniel, you've been thoughtless. What am I to tell our children, Frances and Lucy, about the little boy you've brought here? They're already six and eight and understand more than you imagine. What do you think they'll think of you?"

Parke didn't like being questioned and his high-pitched voice screeched. "You can tell them a fairy tale or something. What does it matter anyway? They'll have dowries and buy proper husbands for it. Lady Frances will see to it."

Jane was indignant. "How can you be so insensitive to your own children? Don't you think the family's reputation counts for anything? Don't you care for them at all?"

Parke was young and impulsive, acting first and thinking about consequences after. He loved his young daughters, but considered them a financial burden and Jane's problem. He'd been away for the years they'd grown from toddlers to little girls. He knew, though, that they were old enough now to begin forming their own opinions. He also knew their opinions likely would be influenced by their mother and grandmother.

Parke responded dismissively. "They are lovely, but girls are of little consequence to a family. If there were boys here it would be different!"

Jane was inconsolable. "If you'd been here these last few years we might have had a boy! Besides, girls need fathers as much as boys, and what sort of father have you been to them?"

Lady Frances couldn't bear to hear this conversation. A woman of nearly sixty, her face reflected traces of her youthful blond beauty. She had an imposing, domineering presence when she was angry.

She spoke directly to Daniel in a determined deep voice, with a trace of English overlaying the typically more relaxed Virginia accent. "Such nonsense! What sort of fool are you, Daniel? Do you think you can go through life incurring debts and the wrath of the world around you? You can't behave here as you would in England. Their customs don't fit Virginia very well. We've worked hard to build family and society here, and though I still value my friends and relations in England, I've never confused the two places. The late Governor Berkeley and I adored your father, Daniel. He was a vestryman and secretary to the Governor's Council. Your father would be unhappy with you today."

Parke never knew how to deal with his mother-in-law. He rose, paced the back of the room and returned to the table. He was naturally tall and seemed to grow taller when he was angry. He pumped his right arm in the air and with tight lips and red face he shouted, "Lady Frances, I know too well the uses of family ties this side of the Atlantic. Jane was married to me for my father's plantation, which she runs to her heart's content. But she cannot run me. I'm a man with my needs and wants, and that I'll pursue."

"Is England any different?" Lady Frances huffed. "Aren't the kings and queens of Europe available for marriage on the basis of who enriches whom? Who do you think you are, to whisk away an Englishman's wife, and to have a child with her? Don't you realize that when I go next to London, a debt will have to be paid for your foolishness?"

"Don't pay it. I will take his challenge and meet him with sword or pistol," Parke curtly responded.

Lady Frances looked Daniel straight in the eye, "I will not have you harm the reputation of our family. You have two wonderful daughters who will wish to be married. Your behavior and debts can harm their chances. I won't stand for it. I'll see to your idiocy now, but I'll not pay your debts forever, Daniel."

With that, Parke stormed out of the house, took a sword and

a pistol, mounted his horse and rode to the nearest tavern, run by Mrs. Applewhite in Jamestown.

Parke drove his horse violently, but soon calmed down to look around. Parke was born in Virginia. When he was eight years old, Nathaniel Bacon had incited the great Jamestown rebellion. Bacon had complained that the Governor was lax in protecting settlers from Indian raids, and the Senecas had come down from New York and staged some. Parke's father supported then-Governor Berkeley against Bacon's marauders. .

With amusement, Parke remembered the adults' arguments and discussions, the excitement of raising militias and arming the town against possible invasion. He'd spent much of his time then playing with wooden swords and shouting military orders to his playmates. He remembered denunciations of Oliver Cromwell and despising the French.

The rebels held their convention, issued their grievances in a written declaration and attacked Virginia's Pamunkey Indians. Governor Berkeley sent Lady Frances to London to plead for Virginia's defense, and she returned with a thousand armed men. By the time she returned, however, the rebellion had already ended, though Bacon's rebels had burned down Jamestown. After that, Sir William Berkeley, then an elderly man of more than seventy, sailed to England to plead to remain as governor and rebuild the town. He died in England before having a chance to make his case.

The next governor, Thomas Culpeper, was a relative of Lady Frances. With Jamestown in ruins, Culpeper stayed with her at Berkeley's great house, Green Spring. As the late governor's widow, Lady Frances inherited Berkeley's house and property, and she willingly rented space to the new governor.

Parke was in England during the so-called Glorious Revolution of 1689, when the English Parliament had expelled King James II and installed William and Mary as joint monarchs. Parke had no particular interest in English politics, and no use for the religious flavor of most English political arguments. Indeed, he steered clear of churches and clergymen. The few he met in England he considered obnoxious and superior, and he detested people who talked down to him. He'd never had to deal with such people in Virginia.

Now he was home again, and the contrast with England was great. Jamestown consisted of about thirty houses. The burgesses had converted an old church that doubled as a jail into a new state house. Mrs. Applewhite's nearby tavern offered beer, rum and some tables to play cards. It was a rough, dark place, and patrons kept their weapons handy.

Parke sat down at a table occupied by several acquaintances from the House of Burgesses and one stranger. They drank rum, and Parke ordered another round for everyone. They were also playing dice for small stakes. Parke anted a few coins and entered the game.

At the table were Major Samuel Swan of Surry, John Armistead of Gloucester and Colonel John West of Nansemond, all three burgesses who held positions in the militia. Parke himself was a colonel, and counted his military designation as higher than the title of burgess. He felt an immediate camaraderie with the three.

"On my ride over, I thought of you, Colonel West. The town is somewhat rebuilt from the rebellion days, but it's no match for London," Parke said.

"Yes, our burgesses had family memories of old London, complete with rats and taxes," Major Swan added. "The Governor had no chance to gain his legislation. Lord Effingham's request was met with shouts and fisticuffs. He had to prorogue the meeting. Governor Culpeper before him fared no better." All of the men at the table laughed as they recalled recent legislative history.

The stranger introduced himself as Mr. Smith from Maryland. He laid out a few coins and the men rolled a few hands of dice. Mr. Smith won at dice most often. Parke suggested they play cards instead, and Mr. Smith immediately produced a deck.

"The new Governor, Andros, seems a different sort than the others," Colonel West said. "He's seen a bit of the world and knows how to negotiate with people who may not agree with him. He reached a treaty with the Indian tribes of New York. He wasn't liked by the Puritans in New England, but he knows the new king well."

Mr. Smith inquired, "Does the new Governor have building plans for Jamestown?"

"We haven't heard any project, though Reverend Blair is planning a new college," Mr. Swan said. "That might mean some more building."

Parke was interested in the news of the new Governor. "What's Andros like? What's his background?"

"He's a military man, a horse cavalryman," Major Swan replied. " He was knighted by the late king for his work as Governor of New York. He's Governor General, not a Lieutenant Governor, and he's imperious. He likes to be announced by twelve trumpets."

All of the men laughed at that.

Mr. Smith asked, "Do we know if the Governor supports the new college?"

Major Swan continued, "The Governor will support the health of the colony. If the college is deemed useful by the burgesses, he'll allow it, but he won't spend moneys aimed at defending the borders for a college."

"Then he'll be at odds with the Reverend Blair," Mr. Smith said while collecting his winnings.

"Who is Reverend Blair?" Parke asked.

Armistead answered. "You must know. He's a Scotsman, sent over by the Bishop of London. After he married Sarah Harrison a few years ago, he was appointed Commissary of the Church of England in Virginia. He collects a salary for that, a dowry from the Harrison's, and he's got his brother Archie over to set up a shop in Middle Plantation. He may not own any land, but he's making himself a wealthy little churchman."

Swan huffed. "Surely you know that Sarah Harrison Blair is a good friend to your dear wife, Jane."

This remark reminded Parke of his recent anger at his mother-in-law. As Mr. Smith raked in a few more coins, Parke shouted, "Let me see those cards."

He looked at the cards and noted that no two were alike on the backs, and that a clever person could have memorized the markings. "Where did you get these cards Mr. Smith? Are they specially made in Maryland?"

"Not at all," said Mr. Smith as he tried to reach for his pistol. He also wore a sword.

Parke had his sword out at Smith's throat. "Why are you here in Virginia?"

Smith answered. "I've just accompanied Governor Nicholson. He's here to meet with Reverend Blair about the college. Governor Nicholson always supports new building projects and education."

Parke thought for a while, holding his sword steady. "Does Governor Andros know that Nicholson is here in Virginia?'

Smith replied. "The meeting doesn't concern him. They're meeting about the Reverend Blair's petition for a college charter to be delivered in London."

Parke continued. "Why doesn't this concern the Governor? The college is for Virginia. We will all be taxed to provide money, land and buildings for it. Why is this so different than building a town? Besides, why does this involve the Governor of Maryland, and not the Governor of Virginia?"

Smith did not reply, but asked "Could you please put down your sword?"

Parke was still furious. "Not now or ever. I think you're a cheat and a spy. You've stolen our money, and you're here to protect a governor of a foreign colony. If you drop your pistol, I'll let you duel with me outside. If you won't, this is your last moment on earth."

Swan, Armistead and West backed away from the table. Smith dropped his pistol, and with a hand on his sword he walked to the door with Parke. Five minutes later Mr. Smith lay dead in the streets of Jamestown, pierced through his chest by Parke. Parke removed the cards and money from Smith's pockets, climbed on his horse and rode home.

***

Daniel Parke felt better. He always enjoyed a fight, and

the argument with Mr. Smith made him forget his anger at his mother-in-law. When he got home, he was relaxed and warmly greeted his father-in-law, Philip Ludwell. He soon described his altercation with Smith and asked, "Is it normal for a sitting governor of another colony to enter Virginia, without first letting the Governor of Virginia know?"

Ludwell had arrived late and didn't hear the earlier conversation between Parke and Lady Frances. He'd since talked to the two women and they wanted him to have a frank talk with Daniel.

Ludwell had been a public servant all his life, but his family required all his negotiating skills. Tall, thin, with thin greying hair, he was in his middle fifties. His two surviving children from his first marriage, Jane Ludwell Parke and teenager Philip Ludwell II, were honest and upstanding, and he was proud of them. Philip worried about Daniel and feared that he was a poor example for young Philip.

"How do you know anything about this Mr. Smith?" Ludwell inquired. "He may just have been frightened by your threat to his safety. People from Maryland may come to Virginia."

"But he accompanied Governor Nicholson, and Governor Andros knows nothing about it," Parke replied. "He says Nicholson is here to see Blair about a college."

"Your anger overwhelms you. You should see the Reverend Blair before you raise any issue with the new governor. Reverend Blair is seeking support to build a college, and Nicholson has always supported educational projects. He's on Blair's board, and Blair will soon be leaving for London to see about a charter from the King and Queen. Now you have publicly killed a man we don't know. Likely the sheriff will come to get you and there will be a hearing before a court."

"Smith was a cheat and the conversation was witnessed. I'm not concerned for myself," Parke said indignantly.

Philip, the Governor of Carolina, offered assistance. "Governor Andros knows I'm here, and we've invited him to dinner next week. You can meet him then and discuss this matter, and hopefully get it quickly dispensed with."

Parke and Ludwell went into the dining room. The children had already eaten and were preparing for bed. Jane and Lady Frances looked at the two men but said nothing. Philip said grace and the dinner followed without argument.

After dinner, Parke decided on a plan. He left the house and walked down to the stables. It was still early evening and a nice warm breeze blew off the river. He checked his largest stallion and his weapons, particularly his long sword. He took the sword in hand and carried it to a small shed where he sharpened it. The weapon was heavier than the piece he normally carried, and he wanted it to be ready for use.

The next day Parke rose early. He dressed in a fine red silk tunic over a gold brocade vest and his plushest peruke, its dark curls billowing well below his shoulders. The Sun King himself wouldn't have cut so frightening a figure. Parke was twenty-six years old, an accomplished swordsman and impetuous.

He mounted his great white horse and rode to the small plantation home of the Reverend James Blair. There he expected to find Francis Nicholson, Governor of Maryland. Though it was morning, a fairly large number of people seemed to be gathered at Blair's home for breakfast. The small stable was full of horses and gear, no doubt belonging to the visitors. A servant came quickly to assist Parke off his horse.

An African servant admitted Parke into the front room. The plantation's furnishings were sparse, but Parke waited, standing, until breakfast finished. Several local planters soon came out of the dining room, including Nicholson and a few Harrisons.

When the full crowd assembled, Parke addressed Nicholson: "Did you receive a letter that I sent you?"

"Yes, I received it."

Nicholson was a short pudgy man in his late forties. Though he'd had a military career and was famous for displaying a short temper, he shied away from personal violence. Nicholson wouldn't have had any chance in a duel with Parke.

Parke continued. "And was it done by a gentleman to send that letter by the hand of a common post to be read by everybody in Virginia? I look upon it as an affront and expect satisfaction." Parke strutted across the front hall of the small house, with a hand on his great sword. His boots made a tremendous clatter on the wood floor.

"Then you must go to Pennsylvania; my hands are tied in Virginia." Nicholson didn't know what Parke was talking about with respect to the letter, but he knew he was being challenged to a duel for his life.

Parke, from the front door, with his hand on his sword, shouted "Come out here!"

Nicholson replied, "Is this your way of giving challenges before so much company? If you have anything to say to me, you know where to find me. I am often in these parts, and you shall never find that I fly the road for you. I am going this afternoon to Sir Edmund Andros. But you shall not catch me making any appointments in Virginia."

Parke stood up and glowered at Nicholson. He seemed to

grow as he pulled his shoulders erect. He stood over Nicholson, who seemed to be cowering.

"How you've changed. You were so used to huff and hector when you were Lord Lieutenant Governor of Virginia. Now that you've met your match you have nothing to say."

Nicholson said nothing, refusing the challenge.

"You're a coward," Parke chided. "I'll let that be known to everyone I know in Maryland and Pennsylvania." He snorted a loud derisive laugh, left Blair's house, mounted his horse and rode off.

That afternoon the Maryland governor visited his Virginia counterpart, mainly to complain about Parke. Andros was already aware of the circumstances surrounding the death of Nicholson's bodyguard, Mr. Smith. Now that he'd been personally challenged by Parke, Nicholson was anxious to make a clear case against Parke to Andros. He took two assistants with him, both well-armed, each on horseback.

At the Jamestown barracks, Nicholson was met by the sheriff, William Roscoe. Since Andros' arrival, William acted both as sheriff and as Secretary to the Governor. William had introduced the new Governor to some of the younger members of the House of Burgesses and a few smaller planters. Though William was not a military man, he admired Andros' decisiveness and attention to administration.

The Virginia Governor heard the arrival of Nicholson's party, and decided to personally greet the guests. Andros was fifty-five years old, and a very fit older man. Not very tall, he had large shoulders and very strong hands. He'd been through many military operations, on land and sea. He'd seen wars in Europe and dealt with skirmishes in New York and New England. His experience could be heard in his loud deep voice, used to command.

When he saw Nicholson, Andros put his hand on his sword and said to Sheriff Roscoe, "Arrest Governor Nicholson and take him into custody. Don't bother with irons, but keep a close watch on him!" This was a public announcement heard by everyone milling in front of the Jamestown courthouse. Nicholson's men were perplexed but, being vastly outnumbered, did nothing.

Nicholson, angered and embarrassed, shouted at Andros, "You can't frighten me. I'm here as a trustee to do the business of the College. You can't stop me from that." With that he marched past Andros into the front hall of the small building that contained the governor's offices, followed by William and two of Andros' armed guards.

Andros followed. Once inside, he signaled two trumpeters to sound a formal fanfare of greeting. The sound of the trumpets reverberated. Ink stands and ink wells, document cabinets, mirrors on the walls all seemed to shake. Everyone's ears rang with pain.

Andros signaled to William that he wished to be left alone with Nicholson, and the sheriff, trumpeters and guards quickly left. The two governors entered a small room with spears and muskets covering two walls. They both sat facing each other, a small round table between them.

Andros spoke first. "Well, Francis, we have lots to talk about." Andros, a little hard of hearing, was enjoying this. He smiled at Nicholson, and thundered "Lovely to be a proper governor again. You should have let me know you were coming. How does it go with Maryland?"

Nicholson, knowing Andros was hard of hearing, shouted, "You call this proper? I come here to report an act of thuggery and murder, and you repay me with an arrest?"

Andros laughed. "But Francis, this is for your protection. Several young burgesses told me this morning that you've lost your bodyguard. It so reminds me of the days in the Dominion of New England. I and our brave men stood our ground waiting for help, and you boarded the first ship to England."

Nicholson grew red in the face, "You went willingly to New England. You were the great governor of the dominion stretching all the way from Maine to the Jerseys. You must have had twenty trumpets then. Did the Puritans love that kind of pomp? You couldn't be in New York at the same time. My decision was sensible. The King was being replaced, and his loyal soldiers should have been in London to see the changeover."

"I would have made it if I could," Andros said. "The Puritans kept me longer than I intended."

"I heard of your suffering," Nicholson said. " To be kept in chains and sent back a prisoner." Nicholson shook his head.

"At my age, such excitement! I was in Rhode Island when news of James' overthrow came to New England," Andros replied. "I dressed as a woman in my only chance to grab a ship. Someone spotted my boots though, and they brought me back to Massachusetts. Marie had passed away by then, and I felt I should do my duty to my sovereign. Have you heard of the Mathers?"

"Yes, they are famous for willingness to let others know that they are the most knowledgeable and moral people on earth. Increase Mather was in London when you were imprisoned. I was sorry to hear the news of your dear wife's passing, but I hear there is a new Lady Andros?"

Andros barely heard what Nicholson was saying. He continued, "What people! We requested the use of a congregational church building and they refused! I restored the celebration of Christmas and they objected. Increase Mather would have the world believe that English soldiers introduced drinking and swearing into Massachusetts. I can tell you, they existed there well before my arrival. Yes, my wife will soon join me, once I've found a house."

"Well, we built some churches in New England, didn't we? " Nicholson loved the opportunity to design towns and commission new buildings. With Andros, Nicholson had been involved in many building projects. He had built the first King's Chapel in Boston, and constructed many Anglican churches in Rhode Island, New York, New Jersey, Maryland and Virginia, most with his own money.

Nicholson now relaxed, and the deep red in his plump face seemed to subside. He and Andros had known each other for years. Nicholson had worked hard to become a royal governor, but he knew that Andros was well aware of his background and weaknesses.

Nicholson was born in Yorkshire, son of a governor of a House of Correction. At the age of twelve, he became a page for the Marquis of Winchester who became his patron. When he was eighteen, he was sent to Flanders to fight in King Charles II's Holland Regiment in the so-called War of Devolution. Nicholson served as a junior ensign in the war to its end.

He saw little military action, and after the war the Holland Regiment was disbanded. Nicholson dropped out of the army for a few years, but rejoined in 1680, and served for a time as a courier in Tangier, where England had sent an army to fight the Moors. He'd never been a high-ranking officer despite political patronage and a military career spanning nearly twenty years. His highest rank was captaincy of a company of foot soldiers.

In 1687 James II created the Dominion of New England and asked Edmund Andros, then Governor of New York, to take the position of Governor. The new dominion stretched from Maine to the Jerseys and included New York. Nicholson was recommended to Andros as an assistant by mutual acquaintances. Andros recalled their first meeting.

"Why did you come as my assistant to the dominion, Francis? You'd never been interested in the colonies before."

"I've always enjoyed being at the creation of the new. You know, I think it's a great service to design towns properly, and build schools and churches. I know I'm not the usual military man, but civilization requires more than just defense."

"Yes, but you've never been a commander of people. Being a governor requires diligence, strength, the ability to make decisions."

"I know, but I felt I could learn on the job. You know, I'm very good at dealing with legislative bodies. I did well in New York, until the riots after the king was overthrown."

"You had your problems with the military side of things. Remember Nova Scotia? All you had to do was recover a fishing boat from the French. How is it you couldn't do that?"

"Well, who can say now? We had trouble finding the boat, though we did try. I imagine some money had changed hands and the French weren't anxious to be found. It was a long voyage for us in those small ships. The French knew they could just wait us out."

"Military targets require a strategy," Andros admonished. "You should have planned how to do it, and taken the resources you needed to accomplish the goal."

Andros was speaking from experience. He'd been a soldier in many military engagements. He'd commanded military actions in Europe, Barbados, New York and New England. He'd become a skilled diplomat and reached peace treaties with the Five Indian Nations in New York, for which he was knighted. New York had been at peace under Andros while Massachusetts suffered death and atrocities due to wars with the Indians. Possibly it was the availability of Andros that persuaded the Board of Trade to join New York, the Jerseys and New England in a single colony.

Andros shifted the conversation. "What is the news of Maryland? How are the people doing?"

Nicholson was honest. "It's a small place but difficult to govern. As you know, I'm a good Anglican and have managed to bring Maryland an Anglican Church Commissary. Our Anglican clergy increased from three to eight. But all this is resented by Roman Catholics and other dissenters. Renegade clergy have issued complaints to the Board of Trade in London, and I have to spend time and energy answering these charges. I have a continually very troublesome government in all respects."

Andros had been Governor of Virginia before Nicholson was officially appointed Governor of Maryland. Before Nicholson arrived, Andros had come to Maryland to conduct the business of the provincial courts there. Andros was very familiar with the problems Nicholson now faced.

"I understand some of your Indians wish to come to Virginia."

"It's a small colony. I don't think it proper for the Indians to be changing colonies as they see fit."

"But they've done that for thousands of years. They see no separation from Maryland to Virginia. We both have an interest in their living in peace without molesting our settlers."

"We try to deal with rebels and cut-throats. What about the warrant for John Coode? Will you honor it?"

"Maryland warrants aren't enforceable in Virginia," Andros said. "John Coode isn't a rebel here."

Nicholson was about to lose his temper, but thought better of it. His face grew red and he stood up and paced around.

"Well, Sir Edmund, we are laying out a new capital city in Maryland. I'll call it Annapolis, after Anne Arundel. Other than that, if you had Mather in Massachusetts, I have my Doctor Bray, the Commissary of the Church of England in Maryland. A single-minded person who seems deaf to reason!"

Andros replied, "So you think our Commissary is better? Are you trying to substitute Blair for Bray?"

Andros was letting Nicholson know that he knew Nicholson wanted to be Governor of Virginia. Nicholson decided to forget about Parke; there was no use further antagonizing Andros. Nicholson took a deep breath, and snorted "Both of them are monosyllables beginning with B."

Andros began to feel a bit agitated. He had some serious business, and for him the issues of defense and the local economy outweighed the building and college projects that interested Nicholson. Andros called for the sheriff and the two trumpeters.

Andros announced, "Governor Nicholson will stay in our

custody for one hour. Please see that he's comfortable." He looked at Nicholson. "We've accomplished much together, but the appropriate rules must be observed. If you come to Virginia, do it formally and let me know in advance. Don't do this again, Francis."

CHAPTER 5

When Governor Andros arrived in Virginia, Philip Ludwell was Governor of Carolina. Since Ludwell had served as secretary to the Governor of Virginia, he decided to invite the new governor to dinner with his family. He meant to treat Andros to a friendly informal welcome to his new post, and Andros gladly accepted.

Andros arrived at Green Spring in full military dress, accompanied by three armed guards. He rode his own horse and wore his most opulent dark peruke. He looked his age but muscular and impressive. On being ushered into Green Spring, he bowed to his host and hostess. "Thank you for your kind invitation. I'm delighted to meet you and your family," he said bowing to Parke and Jane, and the two young girls, Frances and Lucy.

They moved through the huge entry foyer to the dining room, and sat down to a friendly dinner. Lady Frances said to the Governor, "How are you keeping in Virginia? Where are you staying?"

"I'm still at the military barracks in Jamestown, but am looking to rent a house on somewhat higher ground." Lady Frances replied, "A good idea. There are some properties in Middle Plantation. In fact, you are welcome to stay here at Green Spring. We are only visiting, but Green Spring is available for rent if you wish." She said this turning to Jane, "Jane is taking care of our properties, while we are in Carolina."

Since Daniel had been in Europe he'd amassed debts, and Jane had to find new sources of income to support the plantation and the family. Jane smiled quietly at Governor Andros. "You must let me show you the house."

Green Spring was the largest house in Virginia. Built by the late Governor Berkeley in 1649, it encompassed an estate of two thousand acres. The house itself was an imposing two story brick structure with a Mansard roof, a grand entry hall, large ballroom, and extensive dining hall. Though it had suffered greatly when it served as Bacon's headquarters during Bacon's Rebellion of 1677, it was now restored. The house had served as a governor's palace for Governors Berkeley, Culpeper and Effingham. Jane hoped that Andros would be interested in continuing the practice.

"That's very kind of you," Andros said. " I can stay perhaps one night. I must organize a visit to the frontier, as fortifications must be kept. The French likely will be sending Indian raiding parties."

Philip then said grace and asked that dinner be served. It began with a nut soup from an old Powhatan recipe. Local wine was served to all. Frances and Lucy, tired from playing outdoors all day, asked to be excused after they finished their soup. They'd been dressed in their best clothes for the dinner, and found them uncomfortable. Jane excused herself from the table and took them up to their rooms.

By the time Jane returned, oysters were being served. Andros seemed to be enjoying the meal and complimented them on the wine. He was becoming very relaxed, and began a conversation about world affairs.

Andros spoke of his concern for world peace and the threat of France. He said, "The Sun King wishes to preside over everything under the sun. We have our problems in Europe, and their reflection can be seen here. The James River hosted part of the last war with Holland. Six tobacco ships were burned and five taken as prizes. That was a great blow to the King's treasury. The French surely have more designs using the Northern Indians."

Philip was interested. "How do you mean that, Governor? The French aren't neighbors to Virginia, though some believe their Seneca friends attacked frontier settlements during our late rebellion. Poor Jamestown hasn't yet fully recovered from the fire."

The mention of fire brought back terrible memories for Andros. As a young militia man in London, he'd helped to evacuate people from the great fire that engulfed London's docks in 1666. Andros remembered being on horseback and chasing down looters, while rats streamed along the burning docks and streets.

"In Europe, Louis tries to place his relatives on every throne. He's menaced Holland, Belgium and Denmark," Andros said to Philip. "Our new King William wishes to stand against French encroachments."

"And you know the new King well?" Philip asked.

"Yes, we were teenagers together in the Court at the Hague. My family managed to escape from Cromwell's army in the reign of Charles I. My father was Marshall of Ceremonies at the Court in London. When our people in Guernsey were threatened, we returned to the island, as my father was Bailiff of Guernsey. We took refuge in Castle Cornet and rescued many people who feared for their lives. When Guernsey came under Cromwell's siege we made our way to Holland. We were welcomed there by the Queen of Bohemia, the sister to Charles II."

Lady Frances was sympathetic. "Many of us have similar tales to tell. My own family left during Cromwell's reign. I was the youngest, and only a teenager when we arrived here. My father was one of the original patent holders of the Virginia Company, and our property included the Northern Neck. After Lord Berkeley died, my cousin, Thomas Culpeper, served as governor for one year and was awarded the property by the King. The colony has since bought it back, as many freeholders were living on the land."

Andros was curious. "And was your cousin a popular governor?"

"He was a rake and a fool. So was Nathaniel Bacon, the great rebel, who also was my cousin and thought he was going to replace my husband as governor. The Board of Trade seemed to think that the only qualification for Governor of Virginia was to be my relative. Thomas and Lord Effingham came here to enrich themselves, and everyone in Virginia knew it. They both ran afoul of the House of Burgesses. The House asked for Thomas to be removed; they were getting ready to do the same to Effingham, but he went back early to England due to ill health. Francis Nicholson, whom you know, replaced Effingham as Lieutenant Governor for a short while."

"So the Governors didn't get along with the House of Burgesses, and they had to leave because of it?"

Ludwell took that question. "Yes. The House is where all decisions on expenditures are made. As you can imagine, in a small colony, increases in taxation fall on everyone, and many freeholders live close to the edge. If a governor wants to succeed here, he has to convince the House that expenditures are in the interest of everyone. Either that or he'll have to pay for projects out of his own pocket. We live in constant fear of tax revolt. Bacon's rebellion of 1677 ended with the burning of Jamestown."

Daniel, fascinated by the political discussion, raised his glass to the Governor. "We welcome you as a true royalist, your excellency. But times now are bad. Though the Dutch War saw the end of the Navigation Act, tobacco prices are still down. The burgesses haven't much to spend on new projects. We all remember Cromwell's days as days of ruin here. Governor Berkeley was deposed, and spent Cromwell's days here at Green Spring. Cromwell's Navigation Act nearly bankrupted Virginia. Those were awful days for everyone!"

Andros was amused at Parke's tendency to dramatize. "True, Daniel, but I'll never forget the excitement of it. My father said to me, 'Mun, you are the man of the family when I am not with you. See to your mother and your two brothers and sister.' I was twelve years old when we took a boat from the castle in Guernsey to Jersey and then to Holland. My mother wept bitterly. But my father managed to come himself a year later. He died in his own bed in 1674. I've been Bailiff of Guernsey ever since."

The main course of turkey with numerous local vegetables

was served. Andros and Parke opened another bottle of wine. Philip was careful to nurse his first glass, and Lady Berkeley and Jane sat quietly.

Philip addressed Andros. "Some say that Bacon's rebellion here was a reflection of Cromwell's wars in England. Bacon raised a militia of malcontents, issued a popular declaration, and sought to overthrow the governor. After all, the governor stands for the king here. I'm afraid that all of Virginia's politics today are affected by the aftermath of the rebellion. The House will be very careful about taxes and expenditures."

Andros was very interested. "Didn't Bacon couple his complaints with attacks on the local Indians?"

"Yes, and that eventually seemed to be the main cause of the rebellion. Lady Frances went to England and brought back a thousand armed men for the fight, but by then, the rebellion was defeated. Poor Governor Berkeley died soon after. I served as his secretary for a time."

Andros reminisced. "Cromwell did much damage, pitting religions against each other. I just remembered that not long after the restoration, poor old London became engulfed in flames that spread from a bakery on Pudding Street. I was a young fellow then and part of the local militia. We evacuated many, but much of old London burned."

"Well, our fire probably doesn't compare, as Jamestown never had more than twenty or thirty buildings. But our fire was set by rebels. They didn't want anyone but their leader to be governor, and they didn't care to see the burgesses meet either. Bacon died of something he ate, and the rebellion collapsed. Berkeley handled the rebels very severely under martial law, and executed the main leaders. We never held a trial by jury."

"Well, I believe that we should observe the law. People have to feel secure in their homes and businesses. We should keep good records, and make decisions in a timely way. Tell me about the burgesses. Do they take a true interest in the needs of the colony?"

"They represent the freeholders. Virginia's life depends on tobacco. Without it, we would all have starved long ago. The freeholders produce it, and their major concerns are security for the farms and taxation. The burgesses are always suspicious of governors' projects, and generally oppose spending for buildings. They asked for the recall of one governor, almost two, who wanted to build towns and cities. Virginia really has no city life, and people don't see why they should build towns."

Andros laughed. "This is like the Caribbean. I served the Duke of York in Barbados, and got used to a pleasant village life there. I wouldn't have thought to find those ways in Virginia. Certainly New York and Boston are towns, and centers to their colonies."

Lady Frances was impressed with the new Governor, seeing that he'd been so many places and had been Governor in the north before coming to Virginia. "It's taken us a few generations to build up a decent livelihood for our people," she said. "We had two wars and now fifty years of peace with the local Indians. Many Virginia families have Powhatan cousins. Our greatest concern is for the tobacco crop. We have to raise the tobacco, cure it, sell it and deliver it. We have only a few commercial ships, and we need to have contact with the factors in Europe. Many Virginians travel to Europe regularly to see to their businesses. Very few here care much about the indulgences of city life."

Andros raised his glass to Lady Frances. "I feel we have been through wars together Madame. I feel as though we could be brother and sister. Thank you for your kindness this evening. I appreciate your candor in explaining Virginia." Andros then turned to Parke. "I understand you are a burgess. I hope you'll introduce me to your friends in the House of Burgesses."

Parke smiled and poured himself another glass of wine. He offered some to Andros who accepted. Parke then said, "I've recently been to England. The politics of the place are astounding. It's difficult to tell who's up and who's down. Locke's Whigs want to change royal administration of the colonies. What's King William's view of them?"

"The King has a vision of the world, and the colonies are part of it. I'm afraid he expects us to deal with our own security. Would you like to accompany me on the review of the frontier? I have much to learn about the people in Virginia, and you could probably learn much from viewing the colony's defenses."

Parke was delighted with the invitation, and immediately accepted. "Let me show you around Green Spring."

As they walked through the great house, Parke mentioned his meeting with Mr. Smith, and their argument. He built up the story. "He lunged at me and drew a pistol. I responded honorably. We dueled before witnesses outside. And he was here to accompany Governor Nicholson of Maryland. Do you know anything about this?"

Andros had seen many young men like Parke—people who loved their weapons, and used them before considering all the consequences. A young man like Parke would make a suitable aide-de-camp, since he knew the people and issues facing Virginians. He'd also be a proper bodyguard. Andros replied, "It's normally inappropriate for a governor to enter another colony without first informing the sitting Governor. I'll mention this to the sheriff. Probably you should relate your events to the sheriff as well. He'll be with me at the barracks tomorrow."

Andros and Parke agreed to meet at the barracks the next day and to plan the visit to the defenses.

Andros was serious about preparing for Virginia's defenses. He was experienced in defense needs, and England now was at war with France. King William's war began in 1689, the year he had become king. In Europe, battles took place mainly in the Low Countries, where France and Spain attempted to impose their domination. All the rest of Europe, mostly Protestant countries, allied against the French and Spanish.

In North America, the war took the form of the great powers enlisting Indian tribes to attack and harass their opposition. In 1689, Indians attacked the town of Dover, New Hampshire, and massacred half of the fifty inhabitants. A year later, Schenectady, New York was burned to the ground by Indian raiders.

England responded by sending armed forces against Montreal by way of naval expeditions across Lake Champlain. The costs of the expeditions were borne by New York, Connecticut and Massachusetts. King William, busy with the wars in Europe, decided to let the colonies fight their own battles, but he encouraged Andros to support the efforts of New York.

For his defense survey Andros assembled a small group of Virginians: Burgesses Christopher Robinson, John Lightfoot, Thomas West and Daniel Parke. They planned to sail up the James to the Chickahominy River, and from there to the frontier to meet with settlers who lived along the borders. They'd be gone for several weeks, as travel was difficult through the woods along the frontier. Scouts were sent out to tell the settlers of the arrival of the Governor. They were also to visit the site of the Pamunkey village in the Northern Neck of the York River. West, whose mother had been queen of the Pamunkeys, arranged a grand traditional celebration.

Andros was careful to invite several burgesses, as he'd never dealt with a legislative assembly before. He knew that Virginia had been governed by an assembly since 1619, and that elections were widely supported by the public.

The Governor's party was welcomed to farm houses on the outskirts of the western frontier of Henrico County. The settlers welcomed the party with fireworks and a fine community dinner. Andros made it his business to introduce himself to the local clerks and burgesses, who were delighted to meet the King's representative in Virginia.

Everywhere he went he heard the same story. Business was bad, the frontier was vulnerable to attack from the Northern Indians and it would be costly to revive the bulwarks and forts that remained since Bacon's Rebellion of 1677.

Andros inquired of every burgess. "Would it be sensible to provide assistance to New York, as they are on the front line of attack from the French and their Indian allies?" He developed the argument that if the French and Indians could be stopped there, Virginia's own defenses needn't be reinforced in an overly costly manner. Either way defense would be costly. A militia would have to patrol the border regions, and bulwarks restored and maintained. A system of communications and warning systems would have to be established, and kept up to date. Defenses had to include not only militia by land, but ships to patrol the rivers and bays.

The party made their way through the frontier settlements, and a great camaraderie developed between the Governor and the Virginia burgesses. They respected his military experience and knowledge of military planning. He admired their love of their country and their sincerity in wishing to defend it against invaders.

Andros was particularly impressed with the great dinner prepared by the Pamunkey Indians in his honor. John West, now a Burgess, was the son of Queen Cockacoeske, the daughter of the great paramount chief of the Powhatan, Opechancanough. She'd lived with his father, another John West, who was a nephew to the first Governor of Virginia—Thomas West, Lord De La Warr. The senior John West was a great supporter of Governor Berkeley and a hero of the Governor's war to put down the rebellion. In light of this, the House of Burgesses had honored him by exempting him from taxation for life.

The Pamunkeys provided a grand dinner of the finest Powhatan cooking: wild turkey, sweet corn, duck, oysters, blue crab, barbecued sturgeon from the river, and a host of fresh baked breads. Andros understood a bit of Algonquian Indian language from his time as Governor of New York. There he'd negotiated a peace treaty with the five great Indian nations of Northern New York, and had established a close relationship with the Indian chiefs. Indeed, when he'd been Governor of New England, he had to intercede on behalf of Nicholson, then Governor of New York, to settle difficulties with the Indians. While Massachusetts suffered massacres at the hands of the Indians, New York was largely spared.

The visit to the frontier ended with a general agreement

among the group. They would cement their relationship with the local Indians, beef up their defenses to some degree, and ask the House of Burgesses to vote on sending assistance, in the form of money, to New York. They believed that this would satisfy Andros' orders to assist in King William's War, and would also help defend Virginia in a relatively efficient manner.

CHAPTER 6

Blair had earned a master's degree from Edinburgh University and felt close to some of his former professors. They'd taken care of him in difficult times, and Blair thought a college in Virginia, England's wealthiest colony, would add to his prestige and income.

Virginia previously had planned to build a college, and the king had granted a college charter in 1622. The great Indian War of 1622 put an end to the project, and education stayed in the home for the next several generations. The wealthy sent children to Europe for some training, but most learning took place on the plantations. In the family, girls as well as boys learned the basics of reading, writing and arithmetic. Girls were expected to manage the household, which required accounting skills.

Blair needed money for a college, and he badgered everyone he knew in Virginia for contributions. When he left for London, he had the promise of three thousand pounds in support. A parcel of land had been set aside many years earlier for the school, with hopes that construction would be funded through taxes on tobacco revenue. Also, the county surveyor was supposed to contribute some of his earnings toward the college account. These income sources had dried up over the years as settlers began to claim tracts from the land, and tobacco income was down due to the war with France. The surveyor had stopped depositing money in the college account many years before Blair arrived in Virginia.

Blair held meetings with his Board of Trustees, and received some money from supporters, especially Francis Nicholson, who'd been Lieutenant Governor of Virginia before becoming Governor of Maryland. Blair still held a grudge against Nicholson for the failure of Blair's proposed religious courts when Nicholson had been Lieutenant Governor. Blair held personal grudges for a very long time.

Blair needed to go to London to get the college established. He had to get the monarch to renew the college charter, and he needed to find money to support the operation. He discussed his problems with his wife, Sarah, who managed their small plantation in Henrico as well as the college lands.

"I'm off to London to see if I can get us a proper college and a presidency, so we can live in a proper house," Blair announced.

Sarah responded contemptuously. "If you saw to business instead of collecting silly titles, we'd have had a house long ago." Sarah's family was wealthy and her dowry could have bought a proper place, rather than the small plantation they were renting. She'd decided against that in the first years of their marriage. Now after four years, she decided not to help her husband in his strange European projects.

"Will you miss me, Mrs. Blair?"

"I will be fine without you. I have my friends and the running of the plantations. I dare say the servants will miss you more than I ever will."

Blair snarled. "Servants are property. What they miss or don't miss is of no importance. Do you contemplate a life of fornication?"

"I am twenty years old, married to a dour old preacher who loves only boys. What does your religion say to that?"

Blair was angry, but could only sputter. "A life without children in Virginia is likely a long life. You should occupy yourself with more pleasant thoughts and deeds. It's no shame to be married to a Commissary of the Church."

"It's no honor. It doesn't pay the rent and the church of a Scotsman doesn't invite respect—especially one that lives a life of silent sodomy."

Blair shouted. "There is no sodomy in acts with slaves and servants—they are property, and I paid good money for them!"

"I paid the money and I know their misery," Sarah responded. "It's not easy getting people to work hard for their living when their master's a selfish abuser. I hope you have a good long stay in London, and I wish the poor boys of England good fortune in avoiding you."

"This is none of your business. I hope in my absence you will help my brother Archie with his shop. He'll be importing goods from Europe that might be of interest to the ladies."

"How did Archie turn out to be so normal?" Sarah asked. "He cares for other people, in addition to his own son."

"He has a good heart and has been through much. His wife died a year ago, and he's had to raise his son John by himself.

You might want to help him with the boy, introduce him to other children and show him the country."

Sarah huffed. "I'll occupy myself and do my duty. You needn't worry about me. "

"Then, I'll say goodbye," said Blair, turning away. Sarah refused to accompany her husband to the dock. Instead, she planned to visit friends and family in James City.

<hr>

With her husband away on official business, Sarah Harrison Blair was relieved. She knew he'd be gone for a year or longer. She was young and vivacious, and arranged for a busy social schedule of visiting friends and family, as well as a number of parties to be held at her plantation.

Blair left in June 1691. That summer Sarah occupied herself running the plantation and arranging tobacco shipments. She rode out to the fields to supervise the harvesting, and kept the accounts. In the fall, after the harvest, she attended local parties and visited her parents at their plantation.

In early 1692, she visited the plantation of her close friend Jane Ludwell Parke. She was surprised when she arrived. In the parlor was Lady Frances Ludwell, Jane's stepmother, conversing with the sheriff, William Roscoe. Roscoe beamed when seeing Sarah. "You have an air of happiness, Sarah. I'm delighted to see you!"

Philip Ludwell and his son-in-law Daniel Parke entered the parlor to greet Sarah, but it was William who her eyes stayed fixed on. Sarah still felt only warmth and love for William. The young sheriff had since married, and was the father of a new son, but Sarah could tell the desire was mutual from the way he looked back at her.

Lady Frances asked. "Has the Commissary already left for England? I'd wanted him to call on some of my cousins there. They likely would be helpful to him to arrange meetings at court."

Sarah replied, almost joyously, "Yes, he's away on a ship to London to visit with other ministers of the church. I suppose they're like him and will help his business. He left in June, before the summer heat. I could write him, if you wish. He can be reached through Henry Compton, the Bishop of London."

Lady Frances smiled at Sarah. "That would be good for both you and him. A letter like that would let him believe that you are thinking of him."

Jane ordered the servants to take Sarah to her room to rest after her long journey by carriage. She was going to stay for a few days, and then make the journey to her parents, where she'd stay about a week. She planned to spend another week with her brother, Benjamin Harrison III, and his new bride Elizabeth. They'd been married over a year, and had invited her to visit.

Parke, Ludwell and Roscoe discussed the matter of the murder of Mr. Smith. Roscoe asked Parke if he knew Smith, or met him before the duel.

"No," Parke said firmly. "We met in the tavern during a card game. He was clearly a cheat, and this was witnessed by others."

Ludwell added, "The whole episode was well witnessed."

William rubbed his chin and replied, "Yes. But murder in the street is a matter that has to be brought before the proper court. We have a new Governor, and I've been serving as his secretary. He has the reputation of being a stern administrator. He'll have to be informed of this."

"He already knows," Ludwell said. "We told him about it during a visit he made to Green Spring. You probably know that he already met with Governor Nicholson. Perhaps you should informally tell him that you've interviewed Daniel. He'll be pleased to talk with you about it."

"Well, I'll arrange to meet with him soon," William responded. " If all you say is true, there should be no problem. After all, the Governor is the Lord Chief Justice."

The three men rejoined the ladies, who sat looking relaxed and happy. The men began a boisterous conversation about the possibility of a new election for the House of Burgesses. Generally new Governors called for a new assembly, and bestowed gifts of jobs and commissions on people they thought of as supporters. Many planters had children they wanted appointed as clerks and customs agents.

Lady Frances weighed in with a question. "William, will you be running for the House this time? You know the Governor, and many people will want you to represent them."

William long had thought about running, but had been so busy with the Governor's business that he'd done nothing for himself. He was pleased by the flattering inquiry. "Yes. We are at war and our governor is a military man. He deserves a close hearing from the House, and I'd like to serve there."

William was excited, but also tired from a long day. He thanked Jane. "My business is finished. I'll take my leave and thank you for your hospitality."

Jane quickly replied, "It's late, William, and you have a long journey. Stay at least the night and have dinner with us. We have a room prepared for you."

William hesitated; this was the first time in years that he'd seen Sarah. His wife was occupied with their new baby son. "Yes. It's late. I'll stay the night. I wonder if you could show me where I'll be staying, as I'd like to rest a bit before dinner."

Lady Frances was delighted. "That's fine, William. I'll show you to the room." They climbed the stairs. William's room was across the hall from Sarah's, and Sarah heard them as William entered the room.

Sarah thought to herself, "How wonderful to see him again. It's been so long. We have so much to talk about. I could help with his run for the Burgesses."

She was very tired, and lay down on the bed for a short sleep. When she awakened she dressed for a short walk before dinner. The day was bright and cool, a perfect September afternoon, with the trees just beginning to show a little color. As she opened her door, William did the same, and they stood opposite each other, both smiling.

William said, "How are you, Sarah? Have you found some happiness?"

"I'm well enough. I thought to take a walk before dinner."

"May I accompany you? I think our hostess will not mind if we explore the grounds together."

"Of course. I'd be disappointed if you didn't. I know a pretty meadow that's not too far."

They left the house together and walked through the nearby woods to a small clearing near a running brook. William spread his cloak on the ground and Sarah took a seat. They both started talking at the same time, and then both laughed.

They started by exchanging pleasantries, and Sarah finally asked, "Are you serious about the burgesses this time?"

"Yes, though my wife isn't keen. She hates leaving our

plantation and will never come to Jamestown."

"Are you very much in love with her?"

"Not with her, it's always been you."

"You have a family now and a reputation to worry about."

"Do you care for me, Sarah?"

"You know I do, but we have to think this through. I half think that Jane and Lady Frances have arranged that we meet like this. My marriage is a business arrangement, and the Commissary will be away in Europe now for at least a year, maybe longer. I won't miss him, I assure you."

"Well, if I become a burgess, I'll be in Jamestown often. There should be a way for us to see each other without upsetting anyone."

"Let's think about this, William."

William helped her up, and they walked back to the mansion hand in hand. They said little to each other at dinner, but late that evening, after everyone went to bed William knocked on Sarah's door. She let him in and they stayed up for several hours chatting like young teenagers. He ended it by saying, "I must leave early for the town tomorrow, but I wouldn't have missed this evening for anything." Sarah grabbed him and kissed him and whispered, "We have to figure out how to meet again."

<hr/>

Soon after the dinner at the Ludwells', Lady Frances, her husband and some powerful allies quickly began setting a plan in place to get Sheriff Roscoe into the House of Burgesses.

The House was to meet in the following April 1692, and Miles Wills no longer wished to serve as the burgess from Warwick, where William's plantation was located. William knew Wills and went to see him.

The men shared several acquaintances, some of whom served in the House. In fact, Miles Wills had already been contacted by members of the esteemed Ludwell, Custis and Carter families on behalf of young William Roscoe.

Wills liked the young sheriff immediately, and felt comfortable stepping aside and endorsing him for his seat in the House.

Wills made it clear to William that Jamestown took up too much of a planter's time, and that if he wanted the seat, Carter certainly would help him. William agreed; it would have been difficult for Warwick to find anyone else on such short notice, and William had wanted to be a burgess for some time. Carter and Custis sent some men around Warwick who turned enough people up at the Warwick court house to hold the election, and William was elected by voice vote unanimously.

When William arrived in Jamestown he was surprised to be visited at the Governor's offices by Mrs. Tabitha Custis, for whom he'd prepared a customs report at the York pier a few years earlier. She'd told the clerk that she had business with Roscoe and asked to see him alone. She carried a small package with her.

"Congratulations, William. We expect to be proud of you. Mrs. Du Bois, my French Huguenot relative, hasn't forgotten you and asked me to give this to you." William opened the package, which contained a fine wool tunic in dark green, with beautiful brocade edging.

He was impressed and said to Mrs. Custis, "I'm embarrassed. This is so fine. I was only doing my duty. I should return some of the money you gave me. Lord Cavendish was quite drunk with his sailors when I got to Jamestown, and the Clerk of Customs at the port had no time for explanations. He simply took Sarah's report and filed it somewhere."

"As we could have expected! Lord Effingham didn't run a very tight ship. Lord Andros is much the better administrator. I have some business to speak to you about."

William invited Mrs. Custis to sit and he sat down himself. He asked, "Shall I ask a clerk to make notes?"

"No, let's leave this conversation between us. Let me tell you the whole story and you can decide what to do. Several years ago, after my husband, Mr. Brown, died, I inherited his properties as his widow. As we had no children, this is normal under Virginia law. I'd also inherited the properties of Mr. Smart, my first husband, the same way. I knew the family of Mr. Smart quite well, but I never really met any of Mr. Brown's relations who were in England.

"When Nicholson was Lieutenant Governor, a cousin of Mr. Brown, a Miss Elizabeth Davis, came to Virginia with a London lawyer to sue me for the estate of Mr. Brown. He'd left no will. I really don't know her, and I don't know if she is a cousin to Mr. Brown. Apparently in England widows have no rights to inherit property. That's never been the case in Virginia, and many lawyers will tell you that. This Miss Davis claimed to represent herself and an Edmund Brown, who she says is son to Mr. Brown, as rightful heirs to his property. I never knew that my husband had a son in England."

William asked, "What can I do to help? Are these claims before Governor Andros?"

"Well, I don't know. The lawyer is still petitioning courts here, and I think they want a rather large payoff of some kind.

You can decide what to do. I'd like the claim dismissed and ended and will pay you handsomely for your trouble. You can either present it to the Governor—he's the Lord Chief Justice here; or you can introduce a private bill in the House of Burgesses. If you succeed, I'll give you a nice merchant ship. Perhaps the *Pretty Polly*?"

William was surprised and overwhelmed by the offer. A small planter with a merchant ship could hope to become a much larger planter. He was now a burgess and could make deals to increase his land holdings. He was very interested, but knew he needed to talk to someone with a strong head for business. He thought immediately of Sarah.

"I'll help you to the best of my ability, Mrs. Custis. I think I'll take this up with the Governor the first chance I get. He's still new here and very busy now. If I'm unable to do anything before then, I'll see how to handle this in the House."

"Thank you, William. I wish you a successful planting season. Perhaps you can come to dinner some time and bring your wife."

"That's kind of you to ask. I'd be delighted and see if my wife will come. She has a deep aversion to travel. You know that travel can be harsh and dangerous in many places in Virginia."

Mrs. Custis stood and shook Roscoe's hand and left.

Governor Andros had made it his top priority to see to Virginia's defenses. Now William served as his secretary for domestic matters, and Daniel Parke as a military aide-de-camp. Andros concerned himself with visiting local outposts, and spent much of the colony's revenues building fortifications and dredging harbors.

Andros was a hands-on administrator, and personally visited sites as much as possible. William couldn't find an appropriate time to raise an issue about a widow's inheritance before the Governor.

William spoke to the Speaker of the House, Thomas Milner, about the possibility of preparing a private legal bill. Though Mrs. Custis' legal issue hadn't been through the courts, the House of Burgesses served as a court of last resort. It could declare itself as court in session and resolve to hear legal cases. The law relating to the rights of widows was of concern to everyone in Virginia, as death rates were high and virtually every burgess had widows in their immediate or extended families.

In England, a civil case such as the one being brought by Miss Davis would cost a fortune in legal fees and bribes of public officials. It could take years and bankrupt the client. In Virginia, she'd spent her money on transportation for herself and her lawyer, but there were fewer courts and fewer officials to bribe.

In April 1692 William took his seat in the burgesses, one of only eight new members. The House met in a church building; members' offices were in a newly built state house which was still under construction. The Governor's offices were also in the state house.

The full House of Burgesses included 48 members. Some four weren't in attendance due to illness. The House dealt with pressing budget matters first, and generally disposed of its business by voice vote.

William went to lunch and dinner with other burgesses over the next two days, mentioning the case of Virginia widow's rights and what could be done to protect a private person from English litigation. He felt that everyone he spoke to would support a petition to dismiss the claim. He didn't have to offer bribes or business or payments. Everyone in Virginia knew about the plight of widows.

On the third day of the session, William stood and spoke to the House, "My friends in the burgesses, we represent the people of Virginia, and a case of serious importance to all families has been brought to my attention. I request that the House resolve itself to be a court of judicature to hear the case."

Speaker Milner said, "Is there any objection?" Hearing none, he continued, "I declare that this House is now a Court of Judicature, the last appeal available to all persons in Virginia. The Members are advised of their oaths. All personal matters discussed in the walls of the House are private and may not be related or discussed before persons outside this House."

William then related the case of Mrs. Custis facing litigation from Miss Davis of London and her London lawyer. A full debate ensued.

Christopher Robinson of Middlesex: "We've never required a written will from husband to widow. How many of us would have anything if we allowed this kind of litigation? How many of us had widowed mothers? London has too many lawyers."

Francis Mason of Surry: "We've always allowed widows to dispose of their inherited property as they see fit. How can we reduce their rights? There would be no inns, taverns or food shops in Virginia. Will the lawyers of London come over to serve the beer?"

The House laughed and guffawed. Then William Ball of Lancaster, noted in a very professorial manner, "Remember the contract of Mrs. Hannah Bennett Turner Tompkins Arnold? She buried three husbands and kept her farm and property together for her heirs by legal deed. This was never required, but she knew it to be protection for her children."

The Speaker asked, "Is there a motion?"

William responded, "I ask that Miss Davis' claim against the estate of Devereaux Brown, deceased husband of Mrs. Tabitha Custis, be dismissed."

"Is the motion seconded?" A loud shout echoed from all over the church.

"All those in favor of Mr. Roscoe's motion, say aye." The church resounded with loud ayes.

"Any nays?" There were no sounds of nay. The rights of widows aside, no Virginia burgess would support a claim brought by a London lawyer against a well-known Virginia widow, whose current husband was a burgess himself, and whose brother served on the Governor's Council.

Two weeks later, Mrs. Custis again visited William, accompanied by a court clerk. The clerk drew up papers giving title to the *Pretty Polly* to William as payment for services rendered. The ship was docked at a pier in Jamestown.

CHAPTER 7

In early May, William, along with some other newly elected burgesses, was invited to join a celebration at the Parkes at Green Spring. William knew that other new burgesses would attend the celebration, designed to get them to know each other better now that the House was in session. It could last several days, and he expected much beer, gambling and lobbying for favors.

Women were included, but Roscoe's wife back in Warwick never came to Jamestown. She did the daily work of running his plantation while he was away, and showed no interest in his business dealings, either as sheriff or burgess.

William decided that it would be proper to bring a small gift to his hostess. He told his clerk to let the Parkes know he accepted their invitation. He then climbed on his horse and rode to Middle Plantation, where Archie Blair had a small shop selling a variety of items from Europe.

The shop held fabrics and sewing materials, bottles of rum from the Caribbean and farm and kitchen utensils. Archie had found a local toymaker who carved items from wood, and his six-year-old son Jack was busy looking at a few new ones.

When he arrived William saw Sarah showing some items off a shelf to Jack. Archie, seeing William, came out from behind a curtain at the rear of the store to greet him.

"Welcome to our shop, Sheriff! Can I help you with something?"

"Well, I've been invited to Green Spring to the celebration of the beginning of the House session. I'd like to bring something to my hostess, Mrs. Parke."

Sarah said, "If you help me choose a toy for Jack here, I'll help you with that. I know what Jane would like, and she'll appreciate your kindness."

Archie said to William, "I'm thinking of expanding our offerings here. We are the only general shop in Jamestown and Middle Plantation. I get some things from Europe from time to time, but we might do better if I could find some local craftsmen. I'm sure I could sell their things at a price that would make it worth their while."

William thought for a second and then said, "Have you thought of fishing gear? There are many people up in Gloucester who weave their own nets and make implements, but if someone could sell items of greater quality, I'm sure many would be willing to buy such stuff. The same would be true of hunting items."

"Yes. It's quality that people want," Sarah said. "If we could find a good seamstress, many ladies would buy a special gown or hat. I think even the gentlemen would appreciate a finer cut of cloth."

"I have some new items you might like to see," Archie said as he showed Sarah some new bolts of wool fabric, and some new kitchen implements. "They've just arrived on a Dutch ship, and the captain unloaded his cargo very quickly to avoid being impounded by the Governor's guardsmen. Governor Andros means to collect all customs duties and has ordered two warships to patrol the James."

He said this laughingly. He'd obviously gotten a good price for his wares. Sarah and William looked at each other, sharing a fond memory of when William faced down a warship.

"The ship is now in Jamestown harbor," Archie continued, "but the Captain has had some troubles with customs agents before. I think he'd like to sell the ship altogether."

Sarah, well acquainted with the business of shipping goods to Europe, asked "Do you know the captain well? What sort of ship is it?"

"I believe it's quite quick in the water. It's made journeys back and forth from the Caribbean, carrying rum," Archie replied "Captain McForce is just back from a journey to Holland, trading tobacco for goods. He's staying in rooms above Applewhite's Tavern, but will leave to his plantation in the south before long. He lives near Charles Towne. He'd like to dispose of the ship before he goes. He's made quite a small fortune giving the Royal Navy a good chase."

Sarah thought a while. "It's a good business for planters to have their own piers and ships. I've suggested that to my father many times, but he's still of the old school. I may be able to get my brother Benjamin to build a pier and buy a ship. What do you think, William? You're a planter. If you had your own ship, you'd save on shipping costs, and be able to make your own deals. What would you say to that?"

William knew Sarah's head for business was sharper than almost anyone in Jamestown. He finally said. "It takes money to buy a ship." He didn't want to mention that he already owned the *Pretty Polly*. He knew little about ships except that they were expensive to maintain, operate and outfit. Then there was the matter of finding a proper crew, the dangers from pirates and criminals who dealt in trade.

Sarah continued. "But these will be the best circumstances to buy a ship. The owner needs to get rid of it quickly. We know it's seaworthy."

"What are you saying, Sarah? I haven't the money to buy a merchant ship. Times have been very hard."

Sarah said, with Archie looking on, "I can lend you the money, and we can be partners. We can go into Jamestown and draw up legal papers for the purchase and sale. If you don't want to keep your part of it, I'll talk to my brother Benjamin. I think we should go see the captain at Applewhite's soon, before someone else comes up with the money."

William held up a carefully carved wooden wagon on wheels. It was large enough to hold some small boxes, also carefully carved. He showed the toy to Jack, who immediately put it on the floor to try it out. The floor was rough planking but the small toy stayed upright. Jack smiled and said, "This is the one!" Jack looked up at William with a big smile, as if he'd made a new friend.

Sarah showed William one of the new European items, a heavy silk scarf of beautiful floral design. "Jane would love that. I know the color of her new gown and this will set it off beautifully. You should take that, William."

"I can give you a good price," Archie beamed. "I don't know how many people around here will want anything so fine. Would a pound be too much?"

William fished into his pocket for some coins. He'd won them in a card game with some of the other burgesses, and he found enough to make up a pound.

"Come back to my plantation with me, William. I can look over my books and we can talk more about the ship," Sarah said, smiling coyly.

William had been staying in a small room above Mrs. Jones' Tavern, sharing a bed with two other burgesses. The thought of a night away from that room was very appealing. He knew Archie was Sarah's brother-in-law, and he felt that accepting her hospitality as an old friend and potential business partner wouldn't shock anyone.

Archie knew William was considering the appearances of Sarah's invitation and said "Sheriff Roscoe, you're a longtime friend of the family, and it's only proper that some neighbors offer burgesses their hospitality when they're away from home. Please go and have a good night's sleep."

William smiled at Archie. "Thank you for your kindness."

Archie saw Sarah and William to their horses. William tied his horse to Sarah's wagon and helped Archie load some fabric and kitchen items. William then drove the rig back to the Blair plantation. They spent the evening looking at accounts, and William told Sarah about his coming into ownership of the *Pretty Polly*.

Sarah laughed, "You mean you'll own two ships?"

"Yes, and I can't manage either one without you!"

He took her in his arms and said, "We've waited too long to be together. What do you think? Can't we have tonight to enjoy together?"

Sarah smiled, "I thought you'd never say anything. A sheriff and a burgess. What a man you are!"

They spent the night in each other's arms, five years after they'd formally been engaged.

———

The next morning William and Sarah visited Applewhite's and asked to see Captain McForce. The captain was sitting in a corner, sipping some beer, and delighted to see visitors. A very strong and rough-looking man, he was also in very good spirits. When he stood, he was William's height, but clearly outweighed him by over fifty pounds.

After initial greetings, William mentioned his interest in the captain's boat, and how he'd heard it was for sale. McForce happily slapped the table and said, "Come down to the pier. We can have breakfast on her, and you can look her over. I'll show you the fine points."

The party of three rode down to the pier where they were greeted by two of the captain's crew. The captain whispered to one of them, who immediately climbed on board the tall two-masted ship and disappeared below. The ship, the *Adventure*, had obviously seen many adventures. There was clear evidence of cannon shot and musket fire on one side, and one of the sails was being mended by two sailors.

The captain invited Sarah and William below, and they were soon served a fine breakfast of bacon, eggs and porridge and good tea. The large state room held comfortable chairs and a table covered with fine Dutch china dishes and heavy silver cutlery. Maps and various brass implements hung on the mahogany paneled walls. Sarah was impressed by the obvious wealth in the state room. After breakfast, she said, "Can you show us around? How large a cargo can the ship hold?"

The captain noted that it was Sarah who asked the business questions. He said, "If you ship tobacco, she can hold over three hundred hogsheads. She's two hundred tons and carries ten guns for protection." The captain pointed out the locations of the cannons, which seemed clean and in working order. "She's a proper fast brig and takes a crew of six to ten, depending on the route and cargo."

They looked up at the tall masts of this fast merchant brigantine. The ship was about a hundred feet long and twenty-five feet wide. The depth of the hold was about fifteen feet and in very good condition. McForce let Sarah and William look over things by themselves for a while, and various crew members answered questions as they arose.

McForce finally asked, "How do you like her?" Sarah, who was used to bargaining, could tell that McForce didn't want to prolong negotiations. She said, "Where do you live? Are you anxious to get home after such a long journey at sea?"

"I have a small plantation near Charles Towne. It's a very new city, but developing a nice center near the water, and my wife enjoys going into the town. Now that I'm back I suppose we'll build us a town house, and I'm anxious to get going."

After about two hours of further discussion, the three agreed to the sale and the price. They rode back to Jamestown and saw the county clerk who drew up the final papers. The ship was to be sold to William Roscoe who'd refit and rename her. Sarah was to provide the purchase price, which William was to repay over the next year with ten percent interest from the ship's profits.

Captain McForce agreed to move the ship to a pier on the York, where the work of refitting could be done. There, William and Sarah found a small cottage from which they could oversee the work. Sarah saw to her spring planting, but came to the York several days a week to check on the ship's progress. William also returned to his plantation to deal with the planting, and came to the York as often as possible. He told his wife about the brig and she understood he had to be away to see about the refitting. She was used to him being away, and now she was pregnant with their second child.

William named the ship the *Good Fortune.* He had her completely repainted and by the end of the summer she sailed, loaded with tobacco for Holland. William and Sarah spent much time together that summer, and Sarah found an honest factor who paid them a decent price for the tobacco. They were partners and very much in love.

⚓

Sarah decided to visit her brother-in-law's new shop in Middle Plantation. Archie Blair had expected a new batch of English woolen fabric, and Sarah wanted a few new gowns for the fall season.

The small shop stood very near Bruton Parish Church, the only large building in Middle Plantation. People attending services would see Archie's wares, and possibly other shops would follow.

Archie, a medical doctor, was hoping to see an apothecary and a blacksmith follow him. There were few buildings, and everything would have to be built from scratch. Archie expected a new tavern to open just across the road and already had received a shipment of rum and beer from the Caribbean. He was hopeful that business would grow, as more people might move to Middle Plantation. Many burgesses favored moving the capital from Jamestown there, as the land was at a higher elevation and boasted clean fresh water.

Archie welcomed his sister-in-law as she entered the shop. "How happy and fine you look! Do you want to see the new fabrics?"

"Oh, yes, absolutely!" She looked radiant.

He brought out some new tartan wools, a paisley in bright yellow, and some burgundy velvet. Sarah had dark hair, and eyed the velvet. "That would be a splendid winter gown. Would you take three or four yards?"

"Make it five," Sarah said. "I might want a hat or shawl as well."

"And how is my nephew, young Jack? What is he doing today and tomorrow?"

Archie noted, "Well, my dear son is about to help around the shop, but I'm sure I can spare him for something you have planned. How happy you are today? Is there something I should know about? Is James on his way home yet?"

"No, my dear husband is still abroad, but I'm about to visit the West's at the Pamunkey village. They're having a small celebration, and I thought Jack would enjoy a day or two with the Indians."

"That would be fine and a great diversion for him. It's time he got out and saw the country as well. He broods much about the loss of his mother. You're kind to think of him; you're very good with children, you know."

Sarah called to Jack, who had flaming red hair and was full of energy. The six year-old came running and embraced his auntie Sarah. She said, "I have a carriage waiting. We're off to the Wests and the Indians. How about that?"

Jack laughed and ran out to the carriage, without thinking of taking anything with him. Archie and Sarah followed, and Archie threw two wrapped packages into the carriage. "One is for you, and one for Mrs. West. Thank you for this." Sarah replied that they'd be back in two to three days, and off the carriage went.

When they arrived at the West plantation the Indian celebration was just getting started. Foods were being prepared, and in the shade of a large tree stood William Roscoe. He'd arranged to be invited when he knew Sarah was coming. They'd been seeing each other off and on, but had found the Indian village to be the most private place they could meet without stirring up gossip.

William greeted young Jack, "How are we today? How's your wagon doing? Are you going to play some Indian games?"

A number of Pamunkey children had started a game of tag around the south lawn of the house, and William took Jack's hand to introduce him to four boys who were expecting him. Jack ran to the boys joyously, and entered the game without a stop. There were also three little girls who took up the game.

William and Sarah walked up to the house where they were greeted by their hostess, Rachel West. Thomas West, her husband, was the son of John West and the queen of the Pamunkeys, Cockacoeske. He was a very tall muscular man with very dark hair and high cheek bones. Rachel was petite and blond, and a very warm hostess. The family was still close to Indian relatives, and the fall celebration was a kind of Thanksgiving harvest.

"Welcome to both of you," Rachel said "We have a room prepared and little Jack will be sharing a room with the four boys." She took them both to the room where they collapsed in each other's arms. Rachel smiled and said, "Well, I guess we all have something to be thankful for. How are you feeling, Sarah? You look wonderful."

"I never felt better, but I must rest a little now. William will help me with my things, and I have a gift for you from Archie." Rachel smiled, taking the package. "You must send him my thanks for this." Rachel left the room.

"You must sit down. A woman in your condition shouldn't be galloping around the countryside," William said.

"But I feel wonderful, and I have fine news," Sarah said. "I've spoken to my sister-in-law, Elizabeth. She's been married to my brother Benjamin for three years now, and, they are still without child. They desperately want one and have agreed to accept ours. I'll leave in the next few weeks, and stay with them till the baby comes."

William was ecstatic. He had wondered, and worried, what might happen if Sarah birthed a child out of wedlock. The two of them had been together so often since James Blair's departure more than a year ago that it would be obvious the illegitimate child was his. It would be a scandal in the House of Burgesses and a stain on Sarah's name.

"That will be fine resolution," William said with delight. "We can see the child grow up together, even if he doesn't know we are his actual parents. And the Harrisons will have a real Harrison for a child."

Sarah gushed with relief, "Oh, William, I'm so happy. I swore in our contract that I would never marry another and I meant it. You're my only true husband."

"You've been the love of my life as well. Let's enjoy it as much as we can. Who knows what will happen when the great Reverend James Blair returns."

"Nothing will happen. No child will live in his household if I can help it," Sarah declared.

<hr />

The three day celebration went swiftly, and William and Sarah never left each other's side. Jack made good friends with the Indian children, especially one of the little girls. On their return to Middle Plantation, Archie greeted them both with warmth and affection.

"I've received a letter from James. He says his work is going well, and that he hopes to be home by next summer. You'll be happy to hear that, Sarah?"

"Well I've got work to do. And I'll be going to my sister-in-law to help while she awaits a first baby."

Archie smiled. As a medical doctor, he'd seen this look in a woman before. "Yes, I hope all goes well for both mother and babe. If there is any help you need, please remember to ask."

Sarah smiled. She suspected her secret wasn't much of a secret. Archie probably knew or at least suspected. Archie knew his brother was a sodomist and preferred young boys to women. He was also well aware of how close Sarah Blair and William had become, both in business and personally. The following week,

Sarah went to her brother Benjamin's plantation in Charles City. She waited there until the spring. In April, she gave birth to a healthy boy, with dark hair and the characteristic high cheekbones of the Harrisons. Benjamin and Elizabeth Harrison named him, their first-born, Benjamin Harrison IV.

CHAPTER 8

In June 1691, James Blair sailed to London. He brought with him an impressive list of Virginia subscribers and a petition proposed by a joint committee of the House of Burgesses and the Governor's Council requesting the granting of a charter for a new college. The House appropriated money to pay his expenses in England, and he could live comfortably, wherever he wanted.

Blair spent a year rekindling old business and personal relationships and making new connections. London, as it had been when he left, was built around knowing people in power and means.

The political climate had shifted back to being more Anglican. The king, William of Orange, was now a protestant, and willingly accepted by the Church of England. Mary, the queen and daughter of James II, also supported the Church of England. Blair expected the church to be ascendant, and his friends in the church to be helpful. This was the perfect climate for Reverend Blair.

Blair quickly reestablished ties with Henry Compton, the Bishop of London, his mentor and the person who'd sent him to Virginia. They'd corresponded a bit, but hadn't seen each other for six years.

Blair frequently visited Compton at his offices in Lambeth Palace, the headquarters of the Anglican Church in London. Lambeth was a great old castle dating back to 1200. It had been ransacked by Cromwell's troops during the civil war, and restored after the restoration of Charles II. Blair was delighted with the grandeur and obvious wealth of the place.

Compton was a gaunt, formal man. He knew the rules of the church and dutifully followed them. He wasn't a person to appreciate personal possibilities for advancement in a time of upheaval.

Compton had been passed over for the posts of Archbishop of Canterbury and Archbishop of York. Nonetheless, he still had a wide network of supporters and offered sage advice. He coached Blair on how and when to make his proposal for a college in the Virginia colony.

"It would be good if you could make your presentation to the King and Queen sitting together," Compton advised. "But the King has been with his army fighting the French in Flanders. The Queen is well disposed to charitable projects, but you must make your case to the Queen's Privy Council before she'll hear any petition. You'd better show you have money and backing in Virginia before you go to them."

Blair asked, "Will some churchmen be willing to support me?"

Compton said, "Oh yes. Your friend, Gilbert Burnet, is now

Bishop of Salisbury. Remember he lost a position at the Rolls because of a speech on Guy Fawkes Day?"

Blair laughed as he remembered that anxious time, the reason he was now in Virginia.

Burnet, an affable back-slapper of a man, knew his English politics. He recommended to Blair that he wait until an opportune time to petition the King. "Times are hard now, due to the war," he said. " Commerce is down and Treasury expenditures up. You should see if you can collect more in subscriptions and support while you wait for an opportune time. I'd recommend you go down to the Rolls Office and see what your old colleagues might suggest as likely prospects."

Blair spent several months soliciting London merchants who traded in Virginia. He also took Burnet's advice and visited the Rolls Office. There he heard that three pirates who'd plied their trade in Virginia waters were in jail in London. The three men had been captured in 1688 on the James River. They claimed that they were on their way to England to surrender and claim amnesty under a royal proclamation granting pardon to pirates who renounced their trade.

Blair visited the pirates in the London jail, where they lived in luxurious accommodations, and interviewed them. They didn't seem like cut-throats, and he agreed to make a presentation to the Board of Trade on their behalf. The pirates were from Virginia and had tired of the London prison. They were pleased to have a spokesman such as Blair and agreed to pay him for his services.

Blair argued their case successfully, and the Board of Trade released them and restored their goods. In payment, the pirates gave Blair a three-hundred-pound contribution toward the college.

Robert Boyle, the famous chemist, died in 1691 and left 5,400 pounds in his will to be invested and distributed for "pious and charitable uses." Blair met with the executor of the Boyle estate and managed to receive an annual bequest to the college of ninety pounds every year.

Blair waited for nearly another year before presenting the Lords of the Treasury with his petition, in July 1692. He'd rewritten the charter for the college, based on the need "that the Christian Faith be propagate amongst the Western Indians." The Treasury approved the petition in general terms and sent it to the Privy Council. Blair never consulted with any acting or sitting Governor of Virginia or with the Virginia House of Burgesses with respect to specific terms to be granted the college.

In 1693 Blair made a presentation to Queen Mary, sitting alone. The King was still fighting in Europe, and the Queen granted a charter and nearly two thousand pounds in Virginia quitrent tax receipts to fund the college. She also reaffirmed the old terms of the grant of 1622, specifying twenty thousand acres in the Pamunkey Neck and the Blackwater Swamp; a penny per pound tax on tobacco exported from Virginia and Maryland to destinations other than England, Scotland and Wales, and the office of the surveyor's fees and profits.

The charter called for a Board of Trustees that would supervise the building of the college. After the college was erected, general oversight was to be provided by a Board of Visitors, but actual operation of the college was to be conducted by a president and six masters. The first Board of Visitors would include then former Lieutenant Governor Nicholson, four clergymen, four councilors and nine burgesses. Following Scottish, rather than English practice, the college president was chosen from the Board of Visitors. That person would be James Blair.

Blair knew the ins and outs of bureaucracies. He knew that to rise in status, he had to cause someone else to fall. Before Blair left London, he wanted to deal Nicholson a blow. For Blair to collect his appointed salary as president of the new college, it had to be built, and he had to be installed in office. He set about to collect on the promises previously made to him by some of the great planters and Nicholson. Some forty-two planters and clergymen had signed formal subscriptions promising financial support for the college.

⋯

Blair was anxious to return to Virginia and his new post. The trip had been a success and his college a reality. Blair had a list of planters who'd promised money, and he regarded these promises as legal contracts. He aimed to collect on them, by going to court if necessary. He also decided to include in his sermon every Sunday, for the next few months, an appeal and reminder that the college had a charter and must be built, according to the queen's wishes.

By the time he returned to Virginia, Blair had been away more than two years. His small, rented plantation looked luxurious at first, as everything in Virginia looked lush after the sights of London. Upon closer inspection though, the place looked neglected.

The servants greeted him and took his bags, but he detected a certain strange distance from them. They seemed to be smirking, and his wife was away to her brother's. He inquired of his head house servant, a young African slave named William.

"Where is Mrs. Blair, and why is the house so meager?'

William answered. "She is visiting her brother Benjamin, and helping with the new baby, Benjamin Harrison the fourth and latest. After that, she likely will stop and see Mrs. Parke and her parents. She didn't expect you to arrive for another few weeks."

"The plantations seem to be doing poorly, William, Why is that?"

"Prices for tobacco are down, Reverend. All of the planters are doing poorly. The small planters are near starvation, and there is fear of the French and Indians. King William's War rages in the northern colonies."

Blair knew that would make it difficult to collect the pledges of financial support for the college from local farmers. Also, he was irritated that his wife wasn't here to greet him properly, and annoyed that she'd been happily busy with friends and family.

After a few days' rest, Blair rode over to see his brother Archie and to bring him some gifts he'd brought back from London.

Archie greeted him warmly and thanked him for the gifts, which were mostly household items and a few bonnets. Archie had started his shop with a few wares, but now dispensed more than fabrics. He sold home remedies in connection with his medical practice, and various household goods. He'd added fishing and hunting gear, as well as locally carved toys for children. He was pleased that James had brought the bonnets, as that would bring the ladies into his shop. James was boastful about his success abroad.

"I managed to get the charter and promise of financing from

the Queen, though the King was off fighting his war. I will see to collecting the promised subscriptions from planters. It's time we had a college, and I get a house as President."

Archie saw that James was determined, and he knew it was hard to reason with his brother once he'd made up his mind. "Perhaps you should wait before making demands. Times are hard just now, and the new Governor has the support of the burgesses on beefing up defenses. King William's War is also on this side of the Atlantic, don't you know?"

Blair would not hear anything of this. "I'll raise it at the next Council meeting. We'll see about the subscriptions. These people made promises in writing. If need be, I'll raise it in court."

Archie replied, "But the Governor is the Lord Chief Justice here, and the burgesses have already voted for the defenses. Be careful, James. You could be quite alone in this quest. Maybe you should speak to the Harrisons first? They're your family by marriage. It would be wise to gain some allies."

James really didn't understand this conversation. He knew how to wheedle his way through a bureaucracy, and how to manipulate courts through formal proceedings. But he had no instinct for politics. In fact, he looked down on it; he saw himself as righteous and above the rest; it was the duty of the rest of Virginia to do his bidding.

* * *

The members of the Council met in 1693 at the state house in Jamestown. They were ushered in by twenty uniformed soldiers in red tunics, and six trumpeters.

Blair was amazed at how militarized the state house had become. The new Governor took his military responsibilities seriously.

Once seated at the Council table, the Governor welcomed him and asked him to give an invocation.

Blair responded, while the members were trying to retrieve their hearing from the issue of the trumpet blasts. Blair incanted, and then addressed the Council, "I wish to tell you that I have received a charter for a college that would train ministers for the church here. Queen Mary has expressed an interest in erecting a college in Virginia, as Massachusetts already has a college. She also indicated that two thousand pounds from the quitrents should be apportioned to the college, of which I'm to be president."

There was a general murmuring among the Council members. The Governor spoke, "Thank you for the news. I'm sure the college will be a fine investment for the future. The Queen is a warm and charitable person. I've known her since my youth in Holland. Are you aware that England is at war, and that quitrents are for the administration of the colony?"

Blair replied. "The Church wishes to have a full Anglican presence here, and few ministers will come from England, with the death rate so high here, and the lack of churches. The vestries do not keep ministers long enough for them to have a living."

Council member Henry Hartwell chimed in. "Virginia is not England. People live spread out, and there are few cities and churches. The vestries represent the people with money in the countryside, and their first business is to survive. The college will have to do more than train ministers for them to give their support."

Governor Andros added "If we have a charter, we should set about to find a location for the college. We should also put the matter before the House of Burgesses as they will have to raise revenues for it. The regular quitrents have already been spent on defenses."

Blair was surprised to hear of the burgesses spending moneys on defenses. He also was surprised at the efforts of the Governor to buck up the economy in times of stress. Few ships got through due to the war. Governor Andros led the burgesses to establish new industries, so that some manufactures could be made in Virginia. The burgesses passed bills encouraging grist mills and the manufacture of linen cloth. To Blair's chagrin, however, they didn't pass a bill to better provide for Virginia's Anglican ministers.

"I wish Reverend Blair good fortune in his search for support," the Governor said. " It's true that Massachusetts has a college, and I've had dealings with Increase and Cotton Mather, both Harvard men. The training of ministers there hasn't stopped the trials and execution of witches, and murder of Quakers. It would be a good idea for the Virginia vestries to be certain of what they wish in a college."

The Council debated.

Council member Christopher Robinson said, "If there is money, it'll be built. The House of Burgesses needs to be kept informed."

Council member John Lightfoot replied, "It had better provide a practical education for boys of the plantations. For nearly ninety years, the church in England hasn't cared much for our souls. They've been content to send us books to read, hardly a substitute for learned preachers."

Hartwell interjected, "Reverend Godwin was here, and he raised a wonderful crowd with provocative thoughts."

Andros replied, "Morgan Godwin was here?" Morgan Godwin

was a renowned reformist minister and Anglican philosopher.

"Yes," said Council member Charles Scarborough. "He exhorted us to think of Indians and Africans as children of God, the same as us, capable of sitting beside us in church and understanding much the same as us. What do you think of Dr. Godwin, Reverend Blair?"

Blair considered his response, and replied "Mr. Godwin is highly regarded in some circles, but is seen as quite radical in others. God would wish us in Virginia to travel a conservative path."

Scarborough answered, "Well you might say that, with your Harrison dowry, your salary as commissary, and the wealth you accumulate. You have indentured servants and African slaves, same as plantation owners, do you not? Would you say they're just as qualified to sit in a church as you or your dear wife?"

Andros interrupted. "This is not the business of the Council. I'm a good Anglican and respect the church. It's a pleasure to sit in an English colony that respects the King and his religion."

Andros then spoke to Blair. "Thank you for your contribution to this meeting. I support the Church, and plan to give the Church a silver platen embossed with the Governor's coat of arms."

Blair was surprised by the announcement, and thanked the Governor. As the Council meeting ended, Blair left somewhat confused. The Governor was an Anglican and came to church, but he didn't see the Church or the college as a priority. Blair couldn't understand a governor separating the needs of defense from the needs of religion. For Blair, the world was a hierarchy, and religion was the glue that held it all together. He thought it preposterous that a governor would spend the colony's quitrents on the military, while donating only a silver plate to the church.

CHAPTER 9

Benjamin Harrison II, Sarah Blair's father, was delighted to have a great celebration at his home in Surry. In July, the farms were planted and there was time to have some respite from the daily worries of an agricultural colony in a time of war. His son-in-law had finally returned home, apparently with a charter for a new college. Best of all, his son was the new father of the family namesake. Benjamin Harrison II was absolutely delighted with the arrival of Benjamin Harrison IV.

Invited to the weekend celebration were the leading members of the Council and close compatriots in the House of Burgesses. All of the guests would stay the weekend in the great house and adjoining buildings. There would be non-stop food and drink, entertainments, games for the children, music, dancing and, in the evening, fireworks.

Over a hundred guests arrived early on a Thursday afternoon. They included the Ludwells, Jane and Daniel Parke, William

Roscoe, William Byrd I, John and Tabitha Custis, Robert Carter, Richard Lee, Samuel Swann and their families. Children above the age of ten were included, and games were provided for them. The teenagers all looked forward to the music and dancing. Friday evening would be the first ball for many of the young ladies. Harrison had invited the Governor, and expected him to stay through Friday and Saturday. The weekend would end at the local church for a special service to be conducted by the Harrisons' local clergyman, Mr. Smith. Smith was the minister who'd married Sarah Harrison to James Blair, and knew the family well.

Many of the guests of the Harrisons were the same people who'd promised to support Blair's petition for the college. Blair intended to use the occasion to ask them to make good. Sarah was embarrassed that Blair would do this at a family event, and told him so. She left Blair's side as soon as they arrived at her parents' plantation house. There, she sought out Jane Parke, and her brother Benjamin. She looked forward to seeing her *nephew* Benjamin Harrison IV, now three months old.

Blair spotted his father-in-law and greeted him with warmth. The senior Harrison smiled and welcomed the reverend. "Welcome back James. I hope you are here to stay for a while. Tell me about London and the court."

William Byrd and Robert Carter stood nearby and also added their welcomes to Blair. They all had an interest in court politics and looked forward to Blair's stories about the Queen and the Board of Trade.

Blair related to them how he'd managed to get some contributions in addition to their promised subscriptions while he was in London. He expanded on his experiences with the

Robert Boyle estate, which particularly amused Byrd. Byrd was interested in science and knew of Boyle's work with steam. His son, William Byrd II, was in London studying law at the Middle Temple, but Byrd had seen to it that his son received a rounded education in England, including all of the arts and sciences. Carter also knew some math and science, which he used for surveying purposes and evaluating his properties. Carter was intent on accumulating as much land as possible.

"So Boyle will help to educate Virginia?" Byrd mused.

"It's a small bequest but will continue annually," Blair said with pride. "The only proviso is that we establish a school for the Indian children. Once there is a college and faculty, there will be little difficulty complying."

"Yes, but times are difficult now. We may have to wait before the building of a college," Harrison said. "That will take a design, construction and money. Possibly we could start with an Indian school first."

Blair turned indignant. "I've brought back a plan for a college building, designed by Christopher Wren and his colleagues. We'll have to select a building site, but that has also been arranged from the previous plans. It's to be in Middle Plantation."

"True, but that will require the support of the House of Burgesses. They have to appropriate funds for the building. We can help you to talk to the right people, James. The burgesses will be meeting again in October," Harrison said.

Blair thanked his father-in-law, and noted that this year would be the proper time for people to make good on their previous subscriptions. To that, Carter said, "Reverend Blair, be careful. The colony is in harsh times. Promises made to a theoretical charity like the college will have to wait its turn. The colony's defenses must come first."

Blair responded, "The Queen granted the Charter and the quitrents. Subscriptions weren't optional promises. They were legal contracts. They can be enforced by courts."

Carter laughed, "But you are talking about courts in Virginia. Who do you think you'll see sitting as county courts here? Be sensible, and try to be politic with people. No one opposes the college, and no one opposes the Queen. The King is at war and we are in his support."

There was a ringing of bells to come to the main luncheon. The men took leave of each other to search out their families. Blair's face grew red with anger. He was not going to be sidelined by these country bumpkins. He knew his rights and was going to enforce them. After a while, he went back to the luncheon, and sat down next to his mother-in-law. His wife sat next to her brother at the other end of the table.

It was July and so hot that the air itself seemed to boil. Blair, after nearly two years in London, had nearly forgotten the humid, insect-infested Virginia summers. People moved slowly. Work lasted from early light to sunset, a long fifteen-hour day. Blair had also become accustomed to London life, its vibrant commercial center, and the politicking around the King's court and Parliament. London courts were busy with civil and criminal affairs, the commerce of the city was expanding, and life was fun. Jamestown, in contrast, consisted of about thirty small buildings, a newly rebuilt state house, and dusty roads leading to the outlying districts. There was a small church and a few taverns.

The Blair plantation was a half-day's drive by horse and carriage from the Harrison plantation in Surry. Sarah had occupied herself over his two-year absence by running the plantation and visiting and receiving friends and relatives. She kept the accounts relating to tobacco exports and paying taxes, and had invested her dowry carefully, buying up additional land when it became available. The two Blairs had never been close, and James attributed Sarah's indifference to him to her relative youth and the innate stupidity of women.

Blair owned two slaves and four indentured servants, a small number compared to his in-laws and the other great planters. He had no debts, something that would surprise many Virginia planters. Most of them carried heavy debts from year to year, and lived on credit advanced by factors against their tobacco exports.

Blair resolved to visit the sheriff to inquire as to how he could get the college charter enforced, and collect the subscriptions that were earlier promised him. He also petitioned the county clerk in Jamestown to advance him his annual salary as president of the college, a sum of a hundred pounds. Blair believed that he legally held the position, officially approved by the authorities in London. The clerk, confronted by Blair's legal documentation, issued him a note for a hundred pounds, and sent a special notification to the Governor's Council of this action.

Blair next visited sheriff William Roscoe, who was currently also a member of the House of Burgesses. Blair knew that William had once been engaged to marry Sarah Blair, but William could be trusted. He was held in high regard by the Governor and was respected in the community. Blair would need the support of the sheriff if he was to bring anyone to court on debts owed to him.

Blair rode his horse to the court house and requested a meeting with William. He had to wait his turn as there were several people waiting to have wills attested and contracts officiated. After about an hour, William welcomed him into a small room in a small thatched roof building that stood not far from the state house. A court would never meet in a place like this in London.

Blair began, "My dear Sheriff Roscoe, I see you are well and to be congratulated on election to the burgesses."

"Thank you. Congratulations to you as well on receiving a charter for the college. The Council members were surprised that you are already receiving your salary as president."

Blair thought, *The place is so small that everyone knows everything, almost as soon as it happens. They must talk over drinks in the taverns or under trees, who knows? There are no newspapers. London wouldn't allow a press in this colony. Maybe a press would slow them down. With newspapers, they would at least have to wait to read something.*

"The college is taking all my efforts," Blair continued. "We have to plan the construction and location and start the Indian school and hire the professors. All a great deal of work and I've yet to receive any of the quitrents promised by the queen's order. I hope to collect some of the subscriptions promised by Virginians. I have a list of their names and amounts owed here."

Blair handed William a handwritten list. Those subscribers who'd made their payments were marked paid on the document. William looked at the document and asked Blair, "What do you expect me to do with this? It isn't an order of the court. Do you plan to file lawsuits?"

Blair replied, "I have a legal right to these monies. If I have to file a lawsuit and formally testify, I'm prepared to do that."

"Well, the way to do that is to petition the county court to take civil action. They can order that a claim be heard and that the parties appear together before the judge. Perhaps you'd like to do that, but I must tell you, the courts are full of normal civil matters now, and with the colony heavily in debt and preparing for war, this kind of claim will take a long time before it will be heard."

Blair was annoyed at hearing this. He thought about his options, paced the room and came back to face William. William, in his sheriff's tunic, was tall and imposing. He towered over Blair, and William's voice, used to making public announcements, was clear, deep, and easy to hear. But Blair was determined; nothing would convince him he couldn't get his way. He had little respect for Virginians, and knew his way around courts and lawyers.

Blair's shrill, Scottish voice boomed. "Well, I plan to collect the debts owed me. Thank you for the information."

He then stomped out of the room and hastily marched past a line of people waiting to see William. He rode off, and planned his legal complaint. His anger grew as he felt the poverty of his place in the colony, and his inability to exercise power over his own future.

When Blair returned, his wife was away and the servants informed him that two Anglican ministers from relatively outlying vestries were waiting to see him.

Reverends Brown and Wallace were middle-aged men. Reverend Brown was married to a local girl and was the father of three children. Reverend Wallace, like Blair a Scotsman, was younger and not married.

Brown let Wallace do the talking, finally. "My Dear Reverend

Blair, we are here in distress. We beseech you to do something as we are close to starvation in the country. Our parishes have reduced our payments by half as the tobacco is not bringing in the cash the planters hoped for. You must find some monies to supplement us, or we will have to return to London."

Blair, who'd had a bad day already, pleaded, "Please don't be hasty. The House of Burgesses will consider minister salaries in the next session, just a few months from now." Blair was begging them. He couldn't think of what to do. Perhaps he could convince his wife to lend him some cash to cover some of the two clergymen's salaries. He thought again, and knew to himself that she would never hear of it.

Virginia had well over fifty parishes and only twenty ministers to serve them. The loss of two ministers would be terrible for the church and for Blair, personally. Their leaving would be seen as Blair's failure by the Bishop in London. Blair resolved to try to get a loan from his brother Archie, but Archie's business was probably suffering too.

Blair, though on the Governor's Council, did nothing to ingratiate himself with the House of Burgesses. He knew few people there, and didn't know how to deal with them. They were a rough tavern crowd, and sometimes grew too boisterous for his tastes. They talked and talked to all hours, not always to any purpose. Blair knew that many of the planter families were intermarried, and that many of the burgesses were cousins. He never felt that he was part of this extended family. Indeed, he never even felt really safe around Virginia's burgesses.

Blair had some revenues from the early subscribers who

had made good their pledges. In particular, Francis Nicholson had advanced enough monies to begin a grammar school. Blair decided to use those funds to erect a temporary building, and began seeking instructors for the grammar school. The work proceeded slowly, and at every public sermon Blair reminded his parishioners to make their contributions to the new college.

By summer, Blair could think of nothing else to do but bring some claims before the civil courts. Three times he'd asked Robert Carter to make good on his pledge, and three times he'd been turned away. Blair, the third time, right after a Sunday service, was told point blank by one of the Carter children that his father was becoming a little irritated with him. This was said scornfully, in front of half a dozen other people as they were leaving the church. Blair took the remark as an insult.

Virginia county courts met monthly to deal with civil actions. County justices were commissioned by the Governor and appointed with the advice and consent of the Governor's Council. Blair, as member of the Council, had raised the issue of collecting the college's monies, but had been rebuked. Everyone was concerned about defense, and all monies were being spent on new fortifications.

Military garrisons were being established at the falls of rivers. New forest-wise scouting forces were being established along the frontier. This was the first time the western part of the colony had received fortifications and military protection, and their installation was expensive.

Blair took his claim against Robert Carter to the monthly court in Jamestown. From his work for the Rolls in London, he had considerable legal knowledge, and drafted his letter of complaint himself. After waiting his turn, he presented the claim to a lonely judge he'd never seen before. The court house was also empty when he appeared, as no one had come to defend Robert Carter. Only the young teenage Carter boy who'd insulted Blair some weeks earlier sat at the back of the courtroom.

The sheriff called the court to order and the judge, in a proper black robe and wig, sat and formally began by reading the agenda, in the matter of *The College versus Robert Carter*. The judge looked up at Blair and said, "And who represents the college?"

Blair replied, "I do. I am the president of the college, duly appointed by the Board of Trustees."

The judge continued. "But do you have a legal right to represent the college as an institution? Who appointed you to stand in the legal place of the college?"

Blair was flustered. He was the only official of the college, which still hadn't been built. Who else could represent the college in court? "Sir. I am the Commissary of the Church of England, head of the Church in Virginia, and official President of the College to which the Queen has granted a charter. I have the right to represent the college."

"But there is no college," the judge said. " The House of Burgesses hasn't established a college in Virginia, though a site has been set. I believe the House has granted a seat in the burgesses to the college. Who holds the seat?'

Blair again was flustered. Though the college had been granted a seat, it hadn't been filled. The seat was to be elected by the college as an institution, by faculty and students, and trustees. None had yet been selected. "Election hasn't yet been held," Blair admitted.

The judge, irritated, said, "Reverend Blair, the college can have no claim in this court until it exists, and is represented by an official properly selected to serve its interests. That can't be you. You are collecting a salary from the college. You may call yourself president, but if you work for a salary you are an employee. This suit will be seen as self-serving, a way for you to enrich yourself from the pockets of people who are in dire straits and concerned for the defense of the colony in time of war. If you can get the Governor and his council to support this petition, I will hear it. Today you have no standing to bring a lawsuit. This case is dismissed!"

The young Carter boy smiled and shouted "Thank you Uncle William. Father will be pleased."

Blair was astounded. The judge, obviously no lawyer in Blair's estimation, was a brother to Robert Carter, the defendant. Blair couldn't believe that he had no standing to sue, but who would have standing in a court like this? Blair left the courthouse infuriated, but with no avenue to appeal the decision.

Blair took another case before another judge the following month, with the same result. In the second case the judge was only a second cousin to the defendant. It was obvious to Blair that all the subscribers had discussed their legal positions amongst themselves, probably with the cooperation of the Governor, and every court in Virginia would rule the same way. By the fall, Blair had nothing to show for his legal actions.

Near the end of the year, news came from London that the Queen was ill with smallpox. She died by the end of the year, and Blair held a memorial service for her in his Jamestown church. Now his hopes rested only with the King, who was still at war in Europe.

Blair was beside himself with anger and desperation. Seven years after his marriage he still was living off his wife's dowry. His professional path had stalled. Blair was no planter, yet he was living off the wealth of the land. Though he didn't understand trade and commerce, and looked down on people who devoted themselves to trade and profit, it provided him with shelter and sustenance— thanks to his wife's abilities and connections. Blair's allies, those he had left, resided in England.

The power of the government in Virginia resided in the hands of the Governor, who stood for the King, and, in reality was lord of virtually everything. The most powerful burgesses supported him.

Blair resolved to confront the Virginia public and the Governor. He decided to raise the issue in church, and waited until Governor Andros attended.

In early February, Andros attended a service at Blair's church. Andros wore a fine peruke and a black silk military waist coat. The Governor walked with a straight confident gait, but carried no weapon. He projected an image of confidence and authority. He entered from the back of the church and paused to chat and shake hands with many of the burgesses who were waiting for the service to begin. They were delighted and respectful. After all, he was the representative of the King.

A large congregation waited to hear Blair's sermon. He began with some references to the psalms and the Old Testament. He spoke about the morality and the "usual corruptions of mankind." These he listed as ignorance, inconsideration, practical unbelief, impenitence, impiety, and worldly-mindedness. He implored the congregation to be aware of their most serious duty before God: repentance for their sins.

He then looked straight at Andros, seated up front, in a special chair set aside for the Governor. He pounded the pulpit, and with a sharp, almost shrill voice, declared, "The Governor has opposed the building of a college here in Virginia, a project supported by the Queen and the highest authorities of the Church. They who withdraw back and do not put forward their helping hand towards the building of the college will be damned."

Andros was astounded. The congregation mumbled and then there were shouts from the back of the church, "The college is for Blair, not for Virginia!" and "Fie on those who insult the King and his governor!" Some people started stamping their feet, and two young men in the back attempted to lift one of the back benches. In this noise and turmoil, Andros stood up and with a strong military bearing marched out of the church without saying anything. A large number of parishioners followed him.

CHAPTER 10

Edmund Andros was born in London on December 6, 1637 to parents who were low-level nobility. His father, Amice Andros, was the Bailiff of Guernsey and loyal to King Charles I, for whom he served as Marshall of Ceremonies. The king's Marshall of Ceremonies was a military figure who appeared in full dress uniform and organized the ceremonial greetings for visitors to the royal court. Edmund, educated at court along with the other children of the royal household, loved the pomp of the court. He especially loved the sound of trumpets announcing the arrival of the king or other important persons.

The Bailiff of Guernsey acted as Chief Judge and President of the Legislature and the Royal Court in Guernsey. Castle Cornet, where the Andros family lived on Guernsey, had been besieged by forces loyal to Cromwell for nine years.

The Andros family was royalist. Though not actively religious, they supported the Church of England in the English civil wars of the seventeenth century, because the king supported it. They supported the old order, with its emphasis on feudal honor and duty among respected military leaders. They opposed Cromwell not on the basis of religion, but because he was a radical opposed to the old order: Cromwell was anti-bishop, anti-Pope and anti-King. Cromwell and his rump parliament had King Charles I beheaded in 1649.

On a quiet clear night in 1649, Amice Andros put his family on a ship that took them from Guernsey to Jersey, a place still loyal to the king. Edmund was the oldest boy in the family during this escape from the siege, and loyal to his father. He could hear the castle cannon giving the small ship cover.

From Jersey, they made their way to Holland, where Elizabeth Stone Andros, Edmund's mother, joined the court of the Queen of Bohemia, and Edmund met his uncle Thomas Stone, the captain of the Horse Guards. The Queen of Bohemia lived in Holland and was sister to deposed King Charles I.

As a teenager, Edmund befriended William of Orange, who lived in Holland, as well as Mary, daughter of Charles I, who William later married. Amice Andros joined his family in Holland in 1651, along with many other exiles from the court of Charles I.

When Charles II was restored to power in 1660, Edmund Andros returned to England as a member of the Royal Militia. Over the next twenty years he built a distinguished military career. Though not a university graduate, he had strong diplomatic skills and could speak several European languages, including French, German, Dutch and Danish. He was involved in a number of diplomatic missions and was a skilled negotiator.

In 1674 Amice died, and Edmund became Bailiff of

Guernsey. By then he'd married, but had no children. He became a dedicated colonial governor and administrator in Barbados, New York, and New England and was knighted by King James II for his work in achieving a treaty with the Indians when he served as Governor of New York.

Andros had been a good Anglican all his life. He'd built and supported Anglican churches throughout New England, New York and the Jerseys. He expected to do the same in Virginia.

He had terrible memories of dealings with the Puritans in Massachusetts. Like many others of his generation, he also remembered the horrors and bloodshed over differences in religion during the time of Oliver Cromwell. Andros wanted to keep religion out of politics as much as possible. For him, the defenses and economic strength of the colony overrode all other issues.

Now he was being attacked on religious grounds by this foreigner, a Scotsman, who sat on his own Governor's Council. Andros decided to wait and see what authorities in London would do in these circumstances. He wrote to the Board of Trade about Blair. The Board now contained many Whigs, but Scotland was still a foreign country, and the Board knew that Andros was a strong governor and friend of the king.

The Governor's Council in 1693 consisted of six members, including Blair, Daniel Parke, John Lightfoot, Charles Scarborough, Benjamin Harrison II, and Henry Hartwell. Hartwell had been in London when Blair obtained the college charter, and Benjamin Harrison was Blair's father-in-law. They met in a small meeting room in the Governor's offices, in the newly opened Jamestown state house.

The council room had two windows, and there were small tables at each window for clerks who would take the minutes of the meeting. Council members sat around a broad wooden table, each with a quill pen, an ink stand, and two sheets of parchment in front of them. The table held two large candelabras that threw a warm light on the proceedings.

Andros began the meeting by asking Blair to say an invocation. Blair prayed to the Almighty for divine guidance, and ended with a statement that those amongst them who could not support the college were defying the will of London, of God, and of the church which needed ministers in Virginia.

Andros looked straight at Blair and said, "I've received a message from the Board of Trade in London. They tell me that foreigners may not sit on this Council. You are of Scottish birth and a foreigner. I would appreciate it if you would leave without further comment."

Blair ignored Andros' directive and took his seat. He then said, in a loud, piercing voice, "Virginia is a Crown Colony, governed by a king who is head of the Church of England. A governor and his council who do not support the needs of church and clergy defy the will of their masters in London. They will be damned for not supporting the clergy and the college."

Blair continued, "I challenge you on the authority to appoint new ministers of the church. I understand that when I was ill, you had the effrontery to appoint two ministers for James City. Only the Commissary can properly judge the credentials of ministers of religion."

Andros fired back. "I paid them out of my own pocket. I thought you'd complain, so I've asked them to attend this meeting."

Andros asked the clerk to go to the door. Guards then ushered in the two new ministers, Reverends Lewis and Tucker. Andros asked them to explain how they became members of the clergy. Lewis bowed to Tucker, who spoke for both of them, "Why sirs, we took our places as members of the clergy in the same manner as all ministers in Virginia. We are in accord with a directive of the Governor, the representative of the king in Virginia."

Harrison asked them if they knew of any ministers who'd been invested by anyone else, including the Commissary. "No sir, all ministers in Virginia are appointed by the Governor. Perhaps once there is a college and we have more qualified people, the Governor may wish to have assistance with this duty. We are overjoyed that ground had been broken for the new college building, and that thirty thousand bricks have been ordered from Councilor Parke to begin the construction. We thank Councilor Parke for his help with the college construction."

Blair stood and said directly to Andros, "I'm sure Councilor Parke is being paid well for his bricks. I know that you, my excellent governor, are against the church and its ministers. You've opposed the college from the first proposal!"

This was too much for the Council. The members all looked at each other and whispered to each other. Parke and Lightfoot stood up and paced around the back of the room near one of the windows.

Finally, Charles Scarborough in a loud and angry voice, commanded, "Reverend Blair, please leave the room. You are not permitted to be here. You are not of Virginia and don't understand the role of the Governor or his council!"

Parke glowered at Blair, "If you don't go peacefully, we

will throw you out bodily." The three other Council members pounded the large wooden table, shouting for armed guards.

Andros stood, opened the door and motioned to two armed guards who escorted Blair from the Council meeting. On Blair's way out, Andros said in loud firm voice, "Do not return again unless you are officially reinstated by the Board of Trade in London. You are no longer a member of this council!"

Andros was astonished by Blair's behavior. Andros knew his place as governor; he'd been governor in Barbados, New York, New England and now Virginia. He'd served three sovereigns, and was a great supporter of religion, as kings in Europe were always the heads of their established churches. He'd seen in his lifetime the tragedies that come from religious hatred. Virginia was now receiving new non-Anglican immigrants, refugees from religious persecution. Huguenots, expelled from France by Louis XIV, were settling in the southwestern districts. Quakers from the northern colonies were also entering Virginia. Andros felt the colony could absorb new hard-working people, whatever their stated religion. Also, knowing his budget was tight, he simply saw no sense in spending his few resources on cultural and religious projects.

<hr />

Andros was concerned about the Virginia economy. He knew revenues were down due to the hampering of trade by the war— specifically, French and Spanish warships lying along the coast and even threatening internal river traffic. It was difficult for tobacco planters to get their crops to Europe, and without the revival of some kind of trade, many would soon starve.

William Roscoe had tobacco to sell and deliver, and he now

had the use of two ships. The *Good Fortune* was refitted with a few extra guns, and could make a journey along the coast or to the Caribbean. William was no sailor, but he knew many people whose lives depended on boats. They were local fishermen and small traders who navigated Virginia's numerous rivers and inland waterways.

In early September William thought about how he'd handle his tobacco crop, and his two new ships. William was still secretary to the Governor, and entered the Governor's inner office in the new state house, where he found Andros and Daniel Parke in discussion.

Andros was looking over a written claim brought by a London merchant against a Virginia tobacco merchant whose ship had been blown out of the water by a French warship somewhere in the Caribbean. Andros asked Daniel Parke, "How many guns do Virginia merchants carry with them now when they go out to sea?"

Parke responded that he knew a Virginia trader, John Crowe, who owned a ship. Parke said, "Mr. Crowe doesn't believe in guns. He thinks they're too heavy and take up too much cargo space."

"How do you know this, Daniel?" asked Andros.

"Well, I've played cards with him, and he often throws the boat into the pot when he's low on cash. I think he'd like to unload it, and I doubt he ever spent much on armaments for her. I imagine trade is poor and it's expensive to keep up a boat, if it doesn't pay its way. Arming her would be even more expensive."

"What's the name of Crowe's boat?"

"I believe it's called *Revenge* or something like that."

Andros laughed. "That's a well-known name of a French

pirate ship in the Caribbean. The ship I know as *Revenge* was a sloop that carried twenty guns. How can he not have the ship armed?"

William at this point said, "Well, my *Good Fortune* originally had ten guns, but I've refitted her to hold fifteen. The cannons do weigh a bit and affect how fast the ship can go. *Good Fortune* is a sloop, but can handle the guns and cargo pretty well."

Parke was interested, "Have you taken her out yet? Where will she sail, now that the ocean is so dangerous?"

"I don't know. I have licenses for both my ships for commerce. I was thinking of taking my *Pretty Polly* down to Charles Towne, hugging the shore and using inland waterways. There are people moving into Carolina now, and we might be able to strike up a domestic trade with them. We have some linen and gear for fishing and hunting that might carry a decent price. I don't know what we can bring back from Carolina. I was hoping to figure out a normal commerce so I could have one sloop going and the other coming, on a regular schedule. We could also take passengers, though they're small boats and can't take many. I'll have to make a first journey to find out."

"Well, what do you think of a Virginia merchant ship blown out of the water, far away from Virginia waters, being sued by a London customer's lawyer?" Andros never strayed too far from the issue, though William's comments interested him.

Parke said, "My Lord Governor, you are the Lord Chief Justice. You could direct the courts to treat these claims as frivolous, and to be dismissed."

"But we want people to get into commerce and succeed here. The prosperity of the people depends on that. We can't eat our tobacco. Courts have to be open to real claims. They need to be presented with evidence. After all, who lost most here, the party who ordered goods or the party who loaded the ship to be delivered? Has anyone already been paid? We don't know the facts here, and only a court can sift them out. No, I don't think we can summarily decide these things in advance." Andros was a diligent administrator, and he knew his authority in Virginia depended on the perception of him being fair while he kept the interests of Virginians uppermost.

William immediately said, "Yes, my Lord Governor, but London lawyers come here fishing for payments. We have to do something to make it less attractive to them. I imagine the courts in London are so loaded with claims that never see the light of day, that claimants and lawyers think they can reward their English clients better here, whatever the merit of the claim." William was remembering the claim against Mrs. Custis, and how he ended up bringing the matter to the House of Burgesses.

Both Parke and Andros had similar thoughts and spoke nearly at once:

"How do you propose to do that?"

"London has so many lawyers that it's easy to see why they'd bring so many claims here."

"Our laws have always been different than England's to some extent," said William. "We can tell them that anything that happened in the middle of the ocean can't be protected in a Virginia court unless the claimant is a Virginian. That would keep them out of the courts altogether."

"What do you think, Daniel?" said Andros. "Can we just keep them out of our courts altogether?"

Parke didn't know what to say to that. He responded, "I'm in favor of any rule that would keep London lawyers out of our courts, much as I'd like the foreign clergy to go home as well. But that's not the main issue that faces us. We need to promote and protect our trade. We need to get ship-owners to fortify their vessels so they don't lose their livelihoods at sea. We don't have a navy, but we can make our merchant ships carry an appropriate number of guns."

Andros thought about the situation, and said, "Both of you are burgesses. Why don't you raise the issue before the House? A debate about ship fortifications would be a useful exercise. If we can find the cash, maybe we can find the guns we need. You might also raise the issue of whether foreign claimants can sue in Virginia courts for shipments lost at sea."

Andros then turned to William and asked, "When is your voyage planned? I'd like to get a good look at Charles Towne and Carolina."

William was delighted that the Governor would be interested in coming, and quickly said, "Probably we'll be ready in a week or so."

"My mother-in-law and father-in-law are back in Charles Towne now," Parke said. "I'm sure they'd love to have you both stay with them. It's still quite a small place, but a very nice harbor. Lady Frances likes being in the town, as they have a number of new shops and many new people from different places have moved there."

"What sorts of new people?" Andros asked.

"There are native Cherokees, and some Huguenots, Quakers and Jews have come from different parts. Some Germans, Irish and Scots also have come, some from Pennsylvania. Altogether, it's still very small, but everyone is young and anxious to build a new town. My father-in-law has a Jewish doctor, and there is talk about building some large buildings there. They'll have churches of every denomination, if plans go forward."

"It sounds like a little Europe. I wonder if they all speak English, what with the French and the Germans moving in." Andros sounded delighted. "William, we must go and see this new place."

"Certainly, but first I'll have to load the cargo. I was thinking of taking some tobacco, perhaps for trans-shipment to another ship that would go to the Caribbean? The tobacco likely would have a better chance of getting to Europe from there."

Andros thought a minute and then said, "You know, I know some factors in Barbados that might be interested in a triangular trade for tobacco, and possibly rice. I believe that some Carolina plantations raise rice. I'll write to Barbados and see what they think. But let's not wait too long, as it's already September. I believe my stepson Christopher would like to come. He's just sixteen and would make a decent crew member."

"That would be fine with me, said William. Would you like to come, Daniel?"

Parke shook his head. "I'm sorry, but I still have crops to harvest and bricks to burn for construction. I can help you find some crew members if you need them."

❦

William planned his cargo carefully for his first voyage. Sarah mentioned to him that tobacco wasn't bringing in the usual profits because fewer ships were getting through to Europe, not because the Europeans didn't want tobacco. If he could figure a way to get his shipments delivered, he likely could raise the price per barrel to the factors.

His first job was to ask local craftsmen for goods he could take to Carolina. He came up with a mixture of merchandise: fishing gear of every kind, including nets, boots, and baskets. He also had a load of hunting gear, including twenty new flintlock muskets. He added some crates of carved wooden toys, and some barrels of molasses.

The regular crew of the *Pretty Polly* consisted of three fishermen from Gloucester, and two men who'd been crew to Captain McForce of the old *Adventure,* now the *Good Fortune.* William hired his good friend George Harris to be captain. Harris had spent his life on the water as a fisherman. Harris also brought his sixteen year-old nephew, Andrew Morgan. William knew these men personally and trusted them. They had mixed experience, and all knew the local waters.

Daniel Parke recommended two additional men unknown to William. Parke told him that he knew them socially and they'd been crew aboard Crowe's *Revenge*. They were definitely older men compared to the rest of the crew, and rough-looking.

Both of Parke's recruits were French speaking, though not clearly from France. They may have come from somewhere in the Caribbean, as far as William could tell. They spoke very little, though occasionally they whispered to each other in French. The taller man introduced himself as Jacques Couvert. He had numerous tattoos and a small scar on his left cheek just under the eye. The shorter man, Francois Arnaud, was more muscular, and had a graceful, almost aristocratic walk. William was sure these two had never farmed and never fished, but they claimed to know the best routes to Carolina. They planned to find another ship in Charles Towne to take them to the Caribbean, and would work their passage on William's ship rather than pay for it.

Andros came as a passenger. He decided to take six armed guards with him. The guards would handle the ship's guns if necessary. Andros' stepson, Christopher, also came along. He was a tall thin boy, very enthusiastic about the voyage, anxious to help with everything, except climbing to the top of the tall masts.

Mrs. Custis asked William to visit her Huguenot relatives whom he'd met on the shores of the York some years earlier. They'd since moved down to Charles Towne. The Du Boises had started a business making tailored clothing for both ladies and gentlemen. The Bardens were again involved in shipping, mainly to the Caribbean where their four ships had been docked for the last several years. Mrs. Custis gave William a few packages she wanted delivered, three for the Du Boises, two for the Bardens, and long letters for both families.

On the day before the *Pretty Polly* left for Carolina, William went down to the dock to see the last preparations. There he met Sarah, and both went on board to the state room.

Once they were on board, they embraced and held each other for a long moment. They hadn't seen each other much in the last several months. William had been busy with the Governor's business, the burgesses and the boat preparations. Sarah had been out to her brother's plantation to help with the baby as much as she could manage. Now that Blair was back, she had to be careful about appearances.

"How we've changed these last months. You've grown broad in the shoulders. Are you carrying and lifting the cargo yourself?" she asked.

"No, but I've been mustering with the guards early in the morning. I can carry a musket, but nobody can really fire these things accurately. They're good only for frightening people. I think we'll be well prepared."

"There's danger not only from foreign ships. Watch for bandits. What do you think of the crew?"

"We should be safe. The Governor has his young Christopher with him and six guardsmen. I don't know about Daniel's two recruits from the *Revenge*. They're two older Frenchmen and rough, but they say they'll jump another ship in Charles Towne. They speak French more than English. Daniel recommended them, so I felt obligated to take them. We should be able to replace them in Charles Towne."

"Be careful of anyone Daniel recommends. He's so deeply in debt to gamblers that you don't know what deal he may have made to get them on a ship. They could be criminals or pirates. "

"I doubt that. They wouldn't want passage on a ship with the Governor and armed guards if they feared the law."

"Be very careful, William. I don't know what I'd do if anything happened to you."

He took her in his arms, saying "Don't worry. It's a short voyage, mostly inland or along the coast, and we have the Governor on board. We'll be back in time for the Wests' feast, and I'll bring you a pretty gift from Charles Towne."

Sarah smiled, but didn't feel relieved.

Early the next morning all passengers and crew assembled, all cargo duly loaded, and the graceful sloop with two tall masts, the *Pretty Polly*, set sail from Jamestown to Charles Towne.

⁂

The early fall journey by schooner from Jamestown to Charles Towne took two days. The route followed the James

River down to the Chesapeake Bay and then turned south to the network of inland bays and rivers that paralleled the shoreline.

Trees along the route showed a little red, and the sky was a deep blue, almost purple. A strong breeze pushed the *Pretty Polly* at a fast clip. On the second day, dark puffy clouds gathered and the sky filled with migrating birds. The two Frenchmen worked very hard to move the ship along as quickly as possible. They'd sailed these waters before, and feared a September hurricane. William stayed on deck throughout the voyage. Though he'd hired his friend as captain, he was the owner, and the Governor was on board.

William was big and strong, but no soldier. He knew many Virginians who thought violence was the only way to get ahead in the world. They gambled and fought, and paraded weapons for everyone to see. William knew that Parke was one of these, and he worried about the two Frenchmen. Privately, he was relieved that Andros had brought armed guardsmen with him.

On the second day, the *Pretty Polly* left the bay and went out into the ocean. After an hour, they were met by an English warship, the *Albemarle*. The *Albemarle* captain shouted, demanding that the *Pretty Polly* identify herself. William watched as George Harris shouted back that the *Pretty Polly*, duly licensed, was on the way to Charles Towne, carrying Governor Andros as a passenger. Andros was on deck and waved to the Albemarle captain, who recognized him instantly. Flags waved on both ships and the warship signaled to them to continue the voyage.

Governor Andros enjoyed the voyage immensely. He'd grown up on an island, and had sailed in various places under many different circumstances. He also struck up a conversation in French with the two French sailors. Guernsey, where Andros grew up, was just off the French coast. He'd dealt with French-speaking people throughout his youth and enjoyed the memories the sound of French brought back.

When the ship entered Charles Towne Harbor, the sky was dark. The light purple sky of the previous day was now almost black, and the breeze approached gale force. Harris ordered the sails down before the storm reached its height, and only the Frenchmen were willing to scale the tall masts to bring them down. Christopher, Andros' stepson, managed half way up, but became frightened and simply hung to a cross bar until the ship came into port. William was relieved to get to Charles Towne without injury or serious damage.

The two French men were first off the ship. They tied it down with heavy lines, and quickly waved their goodbyes to William. Francois, the short, muscular man, shouted to be heard above the storm, "Thank you for the passage. I hope we'll see you again. Please give our regards to Misters Crowe and Parke." William wished them well. They left quickly and seemed to know where they were going.

After a short while, a coach and six horses with an attached wagon carrying six soldiers approached. The driver introduced himself as David Morris, driver for Carolina Governor Ludwell. He'd come for Governor Andros and his party. William spoke to George Harris. "Someone has to stay here. We'll not be able to unload the cargo until the storm abates."

Harris responded, "Don't worry. I'll stay with Andrew. He's a sturdy boy, very good on his feet, and has been a great help on the voyage. We'll sort out the lines and see that the cargo is ready to go. The rest of the men will find accommodation in the taverns. I spotted two just down the road from here. I promised my sister, Andrew's mother, that I'd keep him away from places that are a bit rough for his age."

William was torn, but he was obligated to accompany the Governor to the Ludwells. Surely, he thought, Parke wouldn't try anything violent in Carolina where his father-in-law was Governor.

Harris and his nephew Andrew watched the crew disembark. William climbed down and just before he entered the coach, he shouted, "I'll be down early tomorrow and we'll see to the cargo. I have some visits to make and packages to deliver. Keep warm and keep watch." Before Andros entered the coach, he spoke to two of his armed guards. He whispered so William didn't overhear.

"Stay nearby with your weapons. Make sure nobody sees you. The captain may need assistance in protecting the cargo." The two guards shook their heads in understanding. Andros climbed into the coach while his two guards found shelter in a small maintenance shed near the pier.

George and Andrew went down to the state room, and prepared a light evening meal. They'd caught some fresh flounder on the way down and fried the succulent fish. They also added some squash and sweet potatoes, just ripe this season. They washed it down with beer, and Andrew promptly announced that he was sleepy, partly from the roll of the ship in the heavy water.

George was amazed at how much the boy slept. George's sister had brought five babies into the world, but only Andrew had grown to be a man. The rest never saw the age of two. Andrew now seemed to be growing out of his clothes as you looked at him. Though his mother worried about him, his father, a Gloucester fisherman, thought it about time Andrew went out into the world.

Andrew was generous to a fault and anxious to please. He was overjoyed to be on this voyage. "Let's have a look in the hold first, make sure everything is dry and secured," Harris said.

"Fine, uncle. Maybe I'll just sleep down there if I find a comfortable place." He was really tired, and didn't move around more than he had to.

They climbed down the narrow ladder to the cargo hold. There they could see the hogsheads of goods, and crates of muskets. The fifteen cannon were in place, but they were not ready to fire, as there hadn't been need for that on the voyage.

Andrew looked at the muskets and took one out to inspect it closely. It was a new variety, and he was curious. "Can I load one to see how it works? It's different than my father's long musket; I think this is a little shorter." George thought the boy had worked hard on the voyage and deserved a little fun. He knew the boy could fire a musket and was interested in these new flintlocks. They took out two muskets, pulled out some shot and gunpowder and prepared them to fire.

"Be careful with them. Any spark could set them off," said George.

They checked the lines and found everything in good working order. Andrew found a blanket and threw it up in a loft area above the molasses barrels. "I'll stay here, Uncle George." He took the musket with him, and climbed a ladder up to the loft. In five minutes he was sound asleep.

George went up to the state room. The ship was still rolling, but the storm abated a bit. Everything hanging from a line banged or clanged, but the clanging was a bit quieter compared to when they'd descended to the cargo hold. George decided he might as well go out on deck to watch. He found a place under the cabin overhang where he was out of sight and sheltered.

He soon heard some quiet conversation, though he couldn't make out who it was and what was being said. He shouted, "Who goes there! Identify yourself!" George still held the musket and quickly readied it for use.

"No need to shout. We're Jacques and Francois. We seek a bit of shelter from the storm and have brought two friends with us."

George pointed his musket. "Get off this ship or I'll fire."

Francois spoke in an elegant French accent. "Let's not be hasty or someone will be hurt. We are here to relieve you of only one of your cannons. Mr. Parke lost it in a card game to Mr. Crowe."

"The cannons belong to Mr. Roscoe, not Mr. Parke. If you take one step further I'll kill you."

George had no intention of letting these pirates near the cargo hold, where Andrew slept, but there were four of them. He let off a shot, which mostly ended up in the air. It was very noisy, creating a bright flash and a lot of smoke. When the smoke cleared George found himself surrounded. Two men he didn't know grabbed his arms and pulled him to a railing on the side of the ship. They had some ropes with them and tied him securely to the rail. The four intruders, led by Francois, then went down to the cargo hold.

George didn't know what was happening when the two

soldiers Andros left behind came on board just a few minutes later. They wore full dress musketeer uniforms, and had pistols drawn. The leader of the two, known to George only as Tom, stopped to untie George. From below, they heard the thunder of another musket shot. George was frightened; he didn't know if Andrew shot the musket or he'd been overpowered too. He feared for the cargo.

George and the two soldiers moved to go down into the cargo hold. As they descended the ladder, they heard the sounds of tussling and boxes being thrown about.

Tom shouted, "In the name of the Governor of Virginia, put down all weapons and step forward." Each of the soldiers held a pistol in one hand and a cutlass in the other. They were both very tall and towered over George, who had no weapon with him.

The hold was cramped with cargo and cannons, and full of smoke from the musket shot. George could barely see what was happening as everything was very dark. He knew where the cargo barrels were located as he and Andrew had just secured all of them downstairs. The cannons were set up along the sides, taking up probably half of the space. Fifteen cannons were more than the *Pretty Polly* was intended to carry.

The cargo was arranged by product and size of barrel. The hogsheads, the largest of the barrels, carried cured tobacco. These were pushed to the back of the hold. Other items were packed in a different size barrels and wooden crates. The crate carrying the muskets had been opened and sat on a large barrel carrying molasses. Only narrow passages were left between the various barrels and the cannons. If the cannons were to be used many heavy barrels and crates would have to be moved.

As he came down the ladder behind the two soldiers, George

looked up to the loft where he last saw Andrew go to sleep. He saw the boy was still there, but Andrew now held his left hand to his right shoulder which was bleeding.

George paid little attention to the pirates. He leaped up on a barrel and from there to the loft. He quickly pulled off Andrew's shirt and fashioned a bandage out of it. He wrapped Andrew's shoulder tightly to stop the bleeding, but he really couldn't see exactly what he was doing. He used his own hand to apply pressure to the wound and the bandage wasn't very well attached. From the loft, both Andrew and George viewed the pirates and soldiers below.

"What happened?" George asked,

"I was asleep till I rolled out of the loft to the floor near the molasses barrel. When I heard footsteps, I hid behind a few crates. It was very dark, especially for them coming down into the hold. They were coming from rain to no light at all. I could see their cutlasses, but they couldn't see anything. I decided to take them by surprise, and fired the musket. It didn't hit anything in particular, but made a lot of noise and flash. Besides being dark down here, we now also had smoke. I moved behind the molasses barrel and pushed it over on them. Two of them got knocked over into the small crates, banging their heads. A small barrel that was sitting on a large hogshead toppled over, knocking both of them out."

Andrew was enjoying telling his story. "They didn't expect it, and the two that came down last starting waving their cutlasses around. They couldn't see what they were doing. Once the molasses barrel had tipped over, it started leaking. The two pirates with the cutlasses started looking for me, and were knocking things over in the process. They just managed to step all over the molasses until they couldn't pick up their feet."

Andrew was laughing. "I tried to get up to the loft but misjudged how big the pirate and how long the cutlass. That's when then I caught the blade in my shoulder." Pointing to one of the pirates whose feet were covered in molasses, Andrew said, "It was him that did it." The pirate still held the blade with Andrew's blood on it. His other comrade was also stuck in the dark room, and the other two were still unconscious on the floor.

Tom pulled up his shoulders still holding his pistols and cutlass. In a loud authoritative voice, he spoke to the pirate pointed out by Andrew, "Where is Mr. Crowe, since you mentioned him? I'm sure the Governor would like a word with someone who would vandalize the Governor's vessel."

The soldiers had heard every word said to George on board deck. The pirates looked at each other, and Francois said, "Mr. Crowe lives in Charles Towne now, and is at his plantation in the country. The Governor of Virginia is not his governor."

"Governor Andros is staying with Governor Ludwell this evening, and they will sort out which court will deal with you. This ship is Virginian, licensed to ship goods. We'll make up a list of damages, and present that to the Governors. They'll decide what needs to be paid to whom. You four will come with us now, to the jailhouse. You've molested this boy, who was minding his own business helping to watch the ship. Is that right?"

Andrew shook his head in agreement.

"We'll find you a doctor. You'd better come with us."

George said, "I have to stay here, and Andrew will be well enough until morning. I'll bind his wound a little better. If you can, please tell William what's happened."

CHAPTER 11

William was impressed—the Ludwell house was comfortable and stately, but not overly lavish. The building was a two-story town home of brick, with a fine garden in the rear. Gilt mirrors hung in the front hall, Persian carpets sat on the tables and floors, and the rooms were warm and comfortable. There were no great stands of weapons and armor, typical of a governor's office in Virginia.

The Ludwells' town house in Charles Towne served as the governor's official residence. The house was located not far from the harbor and was one of many substantial houses built near the center of the town. William noticed on the coach ride that buildings seemed to be going up everywhere.

Lady Frances owned substantial property in Carolina, and the Ludwells also kept a large plantation outside the city. They knew everyone in the colony, and William was very grateful to be able to talk to them about his new business venture.

William wasn't a natural businessman, but he knew his livelihood depended on striking up some business relationships. He tended to trust people too easily, and they often took advantage. In Jamestown, he could talk things over with Sarah who had a sharp business sense and was a hard negotiator. That kind of negotiation escaped William; he simply couldn't haggle over prices, even to his own advantage. He was a person who liked to talk, was persuasive, and basically honest. He was looking for business partners who were like him: people who had something to sell, and were anxious to do it a fair price.

At dinner, Andros' two guardsmen came to the Ludwell residence with the news of the evening's events. William stood when he heard the news. He wanted to go to the ship immediately, but Lady Frances persuaded him to sit down and think about the circumstances. The soldiers assured him that Andrew wasn't hurt badly, and William knew that Charles Towne had some doctors.

Lady Frances handed William a tumbler of rum. "Try this. It will relax you, and I know where you can get some to take back to Jamestown. Merchants think this is the best rum we've had for some time."

William sat down, saying nothing. He was pale and nervous, but listened carefully to the conversation.

Andros remarked that he'd overheard the conversation of the two Frenchmen and knew they were looking over the ship for Mr. Crowe. He said, "I had my suspicions, so I left the two men to see to guarding the vessel. It seems that we were fortunate."

Ludwell remarked. "More than good fortune, that was good planning. I'm surprised that Crowe would be so blatant. He has a decent reputation in Charles Towne, bringing merchandise from the Caribbean. I believe his *Revenge* is still docked here."

"Perhaps he worried about a warship and wanted extra cannon. William, would you sell him one for a good price? You know what you paid for them."

William wasn't sure what to say. He hadn't anticipated selling part of his ship. "I suppose I could. We won't be venturing out far to sea, and should be safe on the way back to Jamestown."

"Perhaps you should think of a suitable arrangement with Crowe," Ludwell said "Take a look at the damage and calculate a price. If he really wants the cannon, add a few pounds extra for it. We'd all be better off if we can reach a quick amicable settlement. I assure you that I'll speak to Daniel about this when I'm next in Jamestown."

Lady Frances chimed in. "William, we'd love to have you down here on regular safe pleasant journeys. I'll give you the names of some merchants who might want your wares. Be sure to tell them that I advised you to see them. I especially recommend Mr. Antoine, whose office faces the harbor. He is honest and very agreeable. He'll tell you everything you need to know about business in Charles Towne. You need to know what's happening to get the best price. Charles Towne has a number of clothiers for men and ladies that follow European styles. The ladies of Jamestown will love the things they make. Also, there are some plantations that will be happy to load up some rice and deerskins for your journey back."

Ludwell then said, "We'll hold a hearing in three days and keep Crowe's men in jail until then. I know that Crowe is in Charles Towne now. You can talk to him at the hearing and make whatever arrangements suit you. Crowe is a good businessman, and I think he'll be an honest fellow under these circumstances."

"Perhaps I should try to see him before the hearing? We might be able to reach a proper arrangement, and complete the details at the time of the hearing. We might need to draw up legal papers."

"I know Crowe well, and you should be careful dealing with him. He's capable of any kind of behavior, and doesn't care if you're a sheriff or any other official," Lady Frances warned. She continued, "For him, business is business. I have him on my list of potential rice sellers. He has a plantation not very far out of town. I'd wait a day before I went out to see him. Wait till he finds out his four men are in the jail here."

Andros couldn't help laughing out loud. "You'll have to tell us everything that transpires. I can't imagine how you get a pirate in his own quarters to agree to a normal business deal selling rice."

Philip laughed as well. "Governors here aren't kings. I'm afraid the real power's in the hands of the planters, pirates and business people. They're the ones who keep the people alive. Everyone who comes here thinks he can make a fortune one way or another, and people are pretty oblivious of the laws and the government. But we know you well, William. If anyone can make a deal with Crowe, it will be you. It's not always that Crowe deals with a sheriff who's also a burgess, especially when four of his men are held in the jail."

William stood up and paced around. He'd listened carefully, and thought through his situation. "I'm grateful for all of your advice. People need to have order to keep business alive. How could anyone make a deal, if everyone suspected everyone else of being a cut-throat? Business has to be regular: willing buyers finding willing sellers. I thank you very much, Lady Frances, for your suggestions, and your comments about Crowe. I expected as much, after seeing his two sailors on the *Pretty Polly*. I'm pleased no greater harm came to anyone, and I'm sure Andrew will love telling tales of his heroism. His mother might not let him go on another voyage after she hears of all of this, though. I never anticipated dealing with Crowe, but I'm here to start a business. I'll see him after I've seen to some other errands, and I'll try to see him before the hearing."

Andros stood and proposed a toast, "Here's to William, George and Andrew! Brave sailors and bringers of business to Charles Towne and Jamestown! I hope your good fortune holds."

William spent an anxious night, and rose early the next morning to go down to the *Pretty Polly*. He took a small wagon led by two horses to the dock. When he got to the ship, he found two of Andros's guardsmen on the top deck while George and Andrew were having a light breakfast in the state room. Andrew looked pale from a loss of blood, but his shoulder seemed decently bandaged.

"Come with me to the Bardons and the Du Boises," William said. "They'll know the doctors in the town, and they'll be honest about how I can start some business here. You remember them from the York."

George laughed. "Yes, you standing on a barrel, shouting at a warship. A good idea—I think Andrew will be happy to leave *Polly* for a bit."

Andrew was looking sleepy again, and said nothing.

They left the ship, climbed into the wagon and went off to the shop of the Du Bois, near the center of the town. Charles

Towne didn't have much of a town center, but it had more shops than Jamestown. The busy port brought a wide variety of merchandise into the town, and a number of merchants did good business.

William noted there was a kind of carefree style about the town. People seemed well-dressed, and very sociable with each other. They verbally greeted each other in the street, and he could hear the sounds of numerous happy conversations.

When he pulled up to the Du Bois shop, Henri and Diane Du Bois came out to greet them. Henri was about Andrew's age, but not as tall or sturdy. He had a dark complexion, and was just starting to develop a moustache. Diane was a very pretty fifteen-year-old, graceful and vivacious. They welcomed him and George and Andrew inside. "We've been waiting for you to come. Mrs. Custis wrote my mother, and she'll be very pleased you made it. She'll want you to stay with us. Please come in."

The shop was small and well-equipped for tailoring clothes for both men and ladies. There were bolts of fabric of a variety of colors, and needles, scissors and threads spread over a broad table. Some gowns hung in a corner, in various stages of completion.

The teenagers already spoke English well, with a slight drawl and a bit of French accent. William thought the speech had a charming musical sound.

"Mrs. Custis sent you some things, including a long letter to your mother," William said. He lifted the three packages and the letter out of the back of the wagon. "I also have some things for the Bardons."

Once inside, William was embraced by Mrs. Du Bois, who grabbed him tightly and kissed him four times, two times on each cheek, French fashion. "Welcome to our shop, William. We are delighted to have you with us." Mrs. Du Bois had dark hair, piled on top of her head, and wore a lovely print and lace dress. She was in her thirties, and youthful in her movements. Diane looked very much like her mother.

William then told them about the events of the last evening on the ship. "I'm grateful nobody was badly hurt, and we should see to Andrew right away," Mrs. Du Bois said. "We know many of the merchants here and can be a help. Also, Pierre Bardon is in shipping and can give you advice on how to deal with Crowe. You must stay with us, at least until the court meets. Mrs. Ludwell will understand. My husband will be insulted if you say no. And we want George and Andrew to stay as well."

William knew his hosts wouldn't take "no" for an answer. And he finally felt he was among friends he could trust. He looked at George and Andrew, and both seemed pleased to have found a haven.

Mrs. Du Bois took Andrew aside and looked at his bandage. "We have a doctor across the street, and we'll see to this now." George and Andrew looked at each other, and George said, "Yes, first things first. He'll be an awful fisherman if he loses an arm. His mother will blame me for it, surely." Andrew laughed and said, "Don't make such a fuss. I'm sure it will be all right."

Mrs. Du Bois put on a cloak, and took Andrew by his good hand. "Come now. I think the doctor's there. If we wait, he'll be away in his wagon to see his patients. You'll like him. He's Spanish and Jewish. We are all unusual in Charles Towne in where we come from. But we're all here to make a better place for ourselves, and get along pretty well."

William said, "We have some business contacts to make that

Lady Frances suggested. I think we'll leave Andrew with you, while we make a few visits. Perhaps we can all see the Bardons together a little later."

"Our house is next door to them near the harbor. Try to get to our place before dark. Henri will go down to tell the Bardons you're here, and we'll have dinner together. It will take at least two days for you to visit the merchants, so it's a good idea for you to get started. Feel free to invite anyone over to our house if you want to talk in a quiet place. Our house is the last one facing the water to the right of the pier."

William and George, using Lady Frances' list of contacts, decided to visit the merchants in the town and show them the hunting and fishing gear. They also planned to see about selling their tobacco in the Charles Towne auction, scheduled for later that week. They hoped to meet with some shippers who dealt in tobacco who carried the crop to Europe via the Caribbean.

The weekly auction of foodstuffs and tobacco was held every Thursday; slave auctions were on Fridays. William decided to visit the tobacco and rice factors first, using the names of people that Lady Frances had provided him.

Charles Towne was still a very new city, with a few residential houses situated on streets near the harbor. The town center consisted of a few small squares surrounding small parks. Near the harbor were some large warehouse buildings used as auction houses. Charles Towne had a bustling harbor with sloops and large three-masted ships, some tied up at piers, others coming and going. There were facilities for ship repairs, and offices of traders and factors, in small wooden buildings along the waterfront.

William and George entered the offices of Mr. Antoine, highly recommended by Lady Frances for dealing with the rice and deerskin trade. A small dark-haired man who seemed to be in a great hurry waved a greeting. He was carrying an armload of documents and motioned to them to sit down. They found a short bench near a table situated in the rear of the small office. Full shelves lined three walls and rolled documents seemed to be everywhere, weighing down the shelves and stacked on the floor in corners.

"Welcome, gentlemen. I am Henri Antoine, at your service. How can I help you?"

The small man held out his hand to shake William's. He seemed to be a jovial fellow, and spoke with a slight French accent, that broadened into a slight drawl.

William smiled. "I'm here with the *Pretty Polly*. I have some cargo to sell and auction, and Lady Frances recommended that I speak to you."

Mr. Antoine looked delighted. "Why, of course. We are to have our rice and tobacco auctions the day after tomorrow. You can unload the merchandise for inspection in the back of this building. We have a warehouse where you can put the barrels and hogsheads, and keep a guard on them if you wish. Have you met any of the other tradesman and merchants yet?"

"We are staying with the Du Boises, and will have dinner with the Bardons this evening. Mr. Crowe owes me a debt, but I've yet to meet him."

"I believe he lunches at the Seafarer Tavern. That's located on the other side of the harbor from here, near where his *Revenge* is docked. If you went at mid-day, you'd find him there."

Mr. Antoine looked a bit nervous when he talked of Mr. Crowe, and William asked, "What do you know about Mr. Crowe. Is he an honest business fellow?"

"I've had no trouble auctioning his rice, but there have been rumors about how he handles the merchandise he brings up from the Caribbean. If he's in your debt, you should have no problem, as he's a very wealthy trader and owns at least four ships that go back and forth all the time. He has some violent men who work for him, and I wouldn't meet him alone. Seeing him at the tavern would be a good idea, and bring your friend with you."

Mr. Antoine pointed to George when he said this. "Be sure of what you ask him for, and stick to what suits you. There are many other traders here who'd like a warm regular relationship with a customer, and who don't favor violent methods. Isn't that what you are looking for?"

William smiled as he felt this man understood him better than he understood himself. William would rather have dealt with cousins, the way most business was done in Virginia. Since he had no cousins in Carolina, he took the advice of the Ludwells, who were like family to him, and of Mrs. Custis, who he thought of as an aunt. The Huguenots treated him as part of their families, and he reciprocated the feeling.

"Thank you for the advice. My name is William Roscoe from Virginia, and this is the Captain of my ship, George Harris. We are very pleased to meet you, and look forward to doing business with you."

"We pay in tobacco notes drawn up by our banker in Amsterdam. The factor representing him will be here on Wednesday to inspect the goods. After the auction he'll provide the notes directly to you. If you wish to use the notes to purchase deerskins or rice, that can be done there at the auction. You can get a good idea of the recent prices by talking to people at the auction or in the taverns. Many of the same people have enough shipping that they come almost every week. In general, rice is now up, tobacco down, unless you find a trans-shipper who can take the tobacco to Europe under a Spanish or French flag. Mr. Crowe has done some trans-shipments, I know. It's a risky business because warships are at sea now; they'll seize or destroy ships they don't recognize."

William looked at George who said, "This seems a good arrangement. I think we'll make up a list of charges for Mr. Crowe, and see what he has to say about the tobacco. Good Virginia tobacco should carry a decent price, if it gets through."

Mr. Antoine laughed his jolly laugh, "Yes, Good Virginia is always in demand in Europe, even in France. It's probably as expensive as jewelry now that shipments are so rare. You should bargain a decent price for good tobacco."

William and George thanked Mr. Antoine and agreed to deliver the hogsheads of tobacco and what was left of the molasses to the warehouse on Wednesday, in time for the auction on Thursday. They'd leave two men to guard the merchandise overnight.

They left Mr. Antoine's offices and went directly to a general store recommended by Lady Frances. They'd brought some of the fishing and hunting gear and carved wooden toys in their wagon. The manager was interested in the goods, but had little shelf space at the moment and wouldn't buy the goods except on consignment. William wouldn't be paid until the merchandise was sold. Since William knew that Archie Blair would likely buy the goods, but at a lower price than he wanted, he decided not to deal with any consignment deals. He did ask the merchant what he would pay for a barrel of molasses, and when he was told five pounds, he revised his estimate of charges to Mr. Crowe.

"Let's have a beer at the Seafarer Tavern," William said to George. " Crowe must know where his men are by now, and the two of us are good enough to handle him and whoever else he has."

They jumped into their wagon and drove the two-horse rig to the Seafarer Tavern. They were surprised when they saw that the tavern was a finer establishment than any in Jamestown. It was bright and offered two glass windows facing the harbor.

They sat in a corner, and shouted to the barman to bring two beers and whatever lunch was on the menu that day. Soon the beers came, followed by a basket of fresh bread and a basket of freshly cooked crabs and oysters.

William asked the barman who served them the beers, "Is Mr. Crowe here? My name is William Roscoe, and I'd like to say hello to him." The server pointed to a table near one of the windows where two men sat, one with great shoulders and a blond complexion; the other was of moderate size but very dark bushy eyebrows.

"I'll tell him you'd like to see him when I take his order." The barman said. He immediately went to Crowe's table, and soon the man with the bushy eyebrows was waving to William and George to join them. William and George carried their beers across the room and sat down at Crowe's table, while the barman transferred their food.

"Welcome to Charles Towne!" said Crowe. "I understand you started your holiday here with great adventure." Crowe was short and dark, but authoritative. He spoke in a low baritone and also seemed to drawl his words. He was friendly, almost jolly.

"We are here on business, and what you call an adventure cost us some goods and repairs," William said.

"Yes, and it's cost me the use of four men, who are now lounging in the jail waiting for a hearing."

"They mentioned your name. One said you felt entitled to one of my guns."

"Silly men! They were drunk, probably, and didn't know what they were saying."

"You can tell that to the court on Friday. Governor Ludwell, with whom I've been staying, will be happy to expedite matters. How much are four men and a cannon worth to you?"

Crowe looked William and George over carefully. The server brought Crowe and the other man two beers, and the same lunch as William and George. "This is Alastair Jackson. He's captain of my *Revenge*, docked just across the way."

William then introduced George as captain of the *Pretty Polly*. "How many guns do you have on *Revenge*? She looks heavy in the water now."

Crowe replied, "Well, you can never have too many guns, with the way warships are about now. We're planning a run to Holland, and I thought I could collect Parke's debt to me from you. You know him well don't you? People say all Virginians are cousins to each other."

"Parke is your Governor's son-in law, and no cousin of mine. Maybe you should take this up with the Governor?"

"That would be inconvenient. I'm sure he'd want us to dispose of this on our own, like gentlemen. What damages did you suffer?"

"Perhaps a hundred pounds of spilled molasses, cleanup, some damage caused by spent musket shells, and most of all a blade injury to George's young nephew Andrew."

"How is the boy?" Crowe seemed really worried.

"He's been taken to a doctor, but he won't have good use of one arm for a while, and he's been a good crew member."

"Perhaps we could make a deal. I know the Amsterdam factor who'll be here on Thursday. I can tell him I'll buy your tobacco at a premium price, and sell you my rice at cost. This is if it all passes inspection."

"It will pass inspection. It's fine Virginia tobacco. I have some other goods—hunting and fishing gear, and some carved wood things."

"How about you throw in one or two cannons?"

William thought this would make this trip easy, but he still hadn't met people with whom he could get into a longstanding business relationship. Next time, Crowe might ask for the rest of the cannons and kill him with them.

"I suppose we could figure a fair price, including the release of your four men from the jail."

"Yes, that's worth a lot, as we want to set sail by next week. How does five hundred pounds sound?"

"You get four men, a cannon and a boatload of tobacco for that?" said George.

William and George exchanged whispers. William said, "A thousand pounds. I'll have to pay my men, and I don't know when I'll make another voyage." A thousand pounds was half the annual salary received by the Governor of Virginia, a princely sum however it was calculated.

"Well, let's not be greedy. I'm taking a great risk in these times. The *Revenge* could be blown out of the water. How about seven hundred and fifty? And if everything works out, we can do this again next year, without the cannon fuss. I can trans-ship to Holland three times a year. I fly a French flag in the Caribbean, switch to a Dutch flag when we're out at sea. Think about it, William."

William considered his choices. He could wait and meet other people, but nobody would have the incentive to pay what Crowe agreed to pay. He wished he could talk this over with Sarah, but she wasn't there. He was on his own and made up his mind. "I suppose that's fair. And we should meet again when you are in Jamestown."

"Absolutely! We are partners now." Crowe raise his beer and said, "A toast to a new business!"

William and George joined him. Both felt relieved to have arranged the sale of the tobacco, but a bit nervous about Crowe as a partner.

William unloaded his wagon at Crowe's warehouse and arranged for the rest of the goods to be delivered the next day. He thought about Crowe's offer all the way to the Ludwells', where he told Lady Frances of his arrangement. He also told her he was staying with the Du Boises, and thanked Lady Frances for her assistance. The two governors were hunting, but were planning on attending the tobacco auction.

It was late afternoon when William made it back to the Du Boises'. Madame Du Bois said to him, "Well, you've been lucky to sell your things, but you still need to meet the businesspeople here. We'll arrange meetings tomorrow through Friday, at lunches and dinners. You'll have met everyone by then. Now stand up. I need to measure you."

William was confused. She said, "Don't say a word. An owner of a ship, a sheriff, and a burgess of Virginia should have a proper suit of clothes. I've already measured brave Andrew, and George is next."

William felt embarrassed, but Madame Du Bois was insistent. "We might have all been blown away by the cannon on that warship, if it weren't for you. I can't understand what makes you so brave. Andrew, too. Don't you think of the danger?"

"Mrs. Du Bois. You are too kind. I was and still am a sheriff. It's my duty to see the laws are enforced. I'm appointed by the Governor, but only after the people of my borough recommended me. In a way I was elected to do what my people expect, and they expect laws to be enforced. Nobody's safe if there's no law and order. It's you and your family who are brave. You left your country and home to board a ship you didn't know, to come to a strange country."

"It isn't bravery to run away from tyranny. We couldn't have stayed in France. The King expelled all Huguenots. We'd have been killed if we stayed."

"Many people came here to escape religious strife," William said. " We've always welcomed people willing to work, regardless of religion. People are building fine businesses and the plantations are growing. We have governors who care for the safety of the people, and we have our own law and courts to hear cases. Virginia and Carolina are good places to start a business. I wish you great success here in Charles Towne. It's becoming a fine city and fine harbor. I hope you find no difficulty with religion here?"

"Carolina seems to be welcoming to all religions. Nobody

hides what they believe. I doubt this is a friendly place for Catholics, as Louis has made war on Protestants. Various groups are talking about building new churches. The Jews are planning to build a temple as well. This will all take time. We have to build up Charles Towne, and we know that trade will be our salvation."

She stopped and looked at William. "We admire you, William, and hope we can contribute to this new place. We still are in your debt, whether you say so or not. What we build is for our children. We hope they can enjoy a religious freedom that doesn't exist in Europe."

William was flattered. "We are all in the same boat now. We have to make room for each other, so long as we're all working hard. If we don't take care of ourselves, there is no one else who'll do it. That's not bravery, its necessity."

A week later William and Andros returned to Jamestown with a ship full of rice, deerskins, and some very fine clothes for men and ladies. William felt he was rich and in business.

CHAPTER 12

Andros had no experience dealing with an elected assembly. In New England he'd refused to let local legislatures meet. He saw his orders as coming directly from his sovereign, the King of England. Andros believed in order, and he'd served many monarchs in good times and bad. He believed the worst times came when there was no clear sovereign, as during the civil wars. The worst sovereign was one who didn't protect the people: the best upheld safety, law and order.

He'd now met most of the leading burgesses, and he knew from what they'd told him that the House of Burgesses was held in high esteem by the people of Virginia. While the normal costs of government were paid for by quitrents, a property tax paid by all landowners in Virginia, expenditures for extraordinary measures had to be voted by the House of Burgesses.

Andros needed additional tax revenues if he was to carry out the orders of the King. Previous governors had run into great difficulty with the burgesses. Lord Culpeper and his successor, Lord Effingham, had faced fierce opposition, never raising taxes to build projects or strengthening the executive. Effingham had been succeeded by Nicholson, who was a temporary appointment as Lieutenant Governor.

Andros was also aware of the aftermath of Bacon's rebellion of 1677. Almost every private conversation he'd held with a burgess or councilor reverted back to the pain of the rebellion. He knew Virginians would oppose unnecessary taxes, and were prepared to revolt and burn down the state house in defense of their livelihood.

Andros hoped to revive a relationship with the burgesses. He'd expended great efforts to get to know young ones like Daniel Parke and William Roscoe. His trip to Charles Towne opened his eyes to the possibilities, if only peace could come to the colonies. Charles Towne was growing rapidly. With peace it could become quite prosperous.

Andros enjoyed the opportunity to speak frankly with Philip Ludwell, who'd served various governors of Virginia and was now Governor of Carolina. He looked forward to spending a few days with Philip and Lady Frances, and seeing the new Carolina territory.

Soon after William had gone to bed that first evening in Charles Towne, Andros expressed shock at the events. He was amazed that the news didn't seem to surprise Ludwell and Lady Frances. Andros asked Philip, "Are there no provisions to safeguard the docks and shipping? It's the livelihood of the people here. How do they do business with the threat of violence so near?"

"You are spoiled, my Lord Governor. Who can or should

protect anyone? We have no standing armies or navies. If the mother country is at war, we occasionally see her warships, but given general behavior on the seas, a merchant ship feels no protection, even if a warship flies his own flag. Flags are easy to make. At sea, it's difficult to tell the law from the pirates. The large shippers have their own men to protect their cargos on land, their own cannon to fight off attacks at sea."

"Yes, I suppose I am spoiled, in that I've always been part of a military order loyal to a sovereign. But we have the same sovereign, do we not?"

"But we have no standing military. Your guardsmen protect you. That's proper; you're a royal governor. There's no English army or navy to protect us. We can call up militias in times of emergency, but the militia men are farmers. If they played at being military all the time, we'd have no crops, no tobacco, and no livelihood. England would collect much less in customs without our tobacco crop to sell. The truth is our people survive by avoiding war wherever possible."

Andros nodded in agreement. "I know, and Europe's wars have a way of finding their way here. Virginians are at war with France as much as the people of New York and the people of England. We'll all have to respond somehow."

"You're a new governor, and it helps to try to see things from the viewpoint of the people living here," Ludwell replied. "Most people here don't seek military conquest; they simply want to survive and hand over some sort of estate to the next generation. The great secret of Virginia and the Indians is not that we vanquished them in war. In proportion, they killed as many as we did. We survived by peace treaty and, though it's embarrassing to say so, by mixing and marrying with them.

There's not a planter family in Virginia without some Powhatan blood. We don't seem to be able to handle our pirates that way. We can't deal with the French that way either."

"You speak of the next generation. What of Daniel? He's a fine military aide. He clearly loves to be seen as a militia man, strutting about with his weapons."

Lady Frances interrupted. "Yes, my Governor, but he lives in two worlds and hasn't adjusted to either one. He spent some years in England, living a grand life of a rich aristocrat. He gambled and saw many ladies, but he couldn't figure the boundaries. There, you have social customs, as well as military men and sheriffs with some power. Daniel doesn't recognize such things. When he's in his element, he knows only what he wants, and cares nothing for anything else."

"He's a good military assistant. He sees the strategy and needs of things, and seems completely loyal."

"He adores you, my Governor, but he doesn't see that you are the executive for Virginia," Lady Frances said. "Daniel never heard of Virginia; he cares nothing for people other than those above him, people he admires. He loves pomp and celebrity."

"Yes. I'm afraid in Virginia that's very dangerous," Philip added. "Though we have no standing military, we have many individuals who see to their own defense. Daniel's debts in England could be handled by a court or an accountant. At least he had the sense when he was in England not to resort to pistol and sword to settle scores. Here, he won't be able to avoid that. He'll have to deal directly with his creditors, and if that's Crowe, it will be Mr. Crowe and a fairly large number of armed men. Murder over gambling debts is pretty widely known in Virginia and no court will touch such cases. Its considered common law, that every person can protect himself and his property, and collect on debts owed him."

Lady Frances added, "Daniel is a brave and loyal boy. He always saw himself as a great cavalier, bestriding the world in military dress. He's certainly a Royalist, as we all are here in Virginia and Carolina. Though he's a burgess, he doesn't seek to represent anyone other than himself."

"How long was he in England, and how did he manage there?"

"He was there for three years, coming back two years ago in 1691. As a Virginian, he had access to a great deal of money, credit against the tobacco crop. He likely was wealthier than most English aristocrats and probably ran up more gambling debts than anyone he knew. He came back with a mistress and a bastard son, who live with him and Jane and the two girls. By coming back he avoided a duel with the husband, and probably some court proceedings."

"It must be difficult for the family, but many couples are separated by travel these days. I've always had my wife with me."

"How does Lady Andros find Virginia?"

"She and her son Christopher find the summers very hot, but they've both settled in well. They have good friends and acquaintances, and love the outlook onto the river. I'm afraid they feel a loss of London life in Jamestown, but London has its disadvantages as well."

Andros continued. "William seems so different than Daniel, more willing to plan for the future and grow his business normally, by meeting customers and the like. I've never been in business myself, but it seems to me the life of the colony depends on getting people to behave like William, and getting more people like him to move here."

"William is a fine, brave fellow, and has been a sheriff for a number of years. He knows the price of law and order breaking down. There are many small plantation owners and tradesmen like him who value law and order over anything else. Others fear the reach of government, and will be quick to riot and cause mayhem if they feel tax laws are unfair."

At that remark, Andros felt comfortable raising the issue of Virginia's House of Burgesses. "I plan to have a new election. What can you tell me about the House of Burgesses?"

Philip paused and then said, "In Virginia taxes are paid by the freeholders who plant tobacco. Taxes are collected in the form of notes on tobacco. Customs duties are imposed on tobacco in the form of a price per pound. There's very little cash in Virginia, and the entire financial system depends on credits estimated on next year's tobacco crop. That's what confuses Daniel. He lives on credit he never sees, so he thinks there's no limit to it. The only limit is next year's crop, and in England, tobacco credits are the same as gold. Not so in Virginia. The House of Burgesses mainly represents the freeholders, and the House is naturally predisposed to oppose most proposals, especially proposals for tax increases. Many people live near the edge, and simply can't afford tax increases. You'll see that when the burgesses meet."

"But I'll have to get some monies from the burgesses if I'm to fulfill the orders of the King. We are at war with France along the northern borders. We need to do something to support the Governor of New York."

Philip and Lady Frances shook their heads. Lady Frances summed up the conversation. "Be generous with them. They aren't stupid. Nobody wants to be overrun by the French and their Indian savages. If you explain your position and offer aid yourself, they'll see things the way you do. Lord Berkeley was governor for forty years, and held the support of the burgesses almost the whole time. I'm sure Virginians are happy to have a governor who thinks of Virginia more than his own pocketbook. You don't know how unusual that is. Culpeper and Effingham were regarded as no better than pirates by the burgesses."

They all had a brief drink before going to bed. Andros felt more confident about his plans. When he returned to Jamestown the following week, he announced to his council that he would order an election for a new House of Burgesses. He'd been governor for a year, and had an agenda that needed a legislative stamp of approval. He needed to convince the burgesses that it was in the interests of the entire colony to support King William in his efforts against Louis XIV.

CHAPTER 13

After the fall crops were harvested, sheriffs all over Virginia rode to the plantations of the various freeholders to announce an open election. Over the latter part of the year, people met in the town squares to openly debate, and the burgesses who knew the state of the colony's defenses expressed their concern.

Elections were great events for the people of Virginia. Towns were few and very small, and elections were an occasion to get together in small town squares, often consisting of only a few houses. Distant neighbors could meet face to face. Food was generally provided by the local business people, and sheriffs made sure that no alcohol was available before the votes were tallied. Voting was generally by hand or voice vote, and Election Day was a day for flag waving, fireworks, and general good cheer.

Andros was pleased to see the people come out in great numbers to select their representatives. He called a meeting of the newly elected House for March 1693.

Governor Andros was a master at avoiding conflict. He gracefully walked that fine line between being a surrogate of England and an advocate for Virginia. He was able to maintain key allies in the House of Burgesses, in part, by showing deference and support to its members.

The newly elected House of Burgesses met in March 1693, with great pomp and ceremony. Uniformed soldiers in red tunics stood outside the small red brick state house. Trumpeters and flag bearers greeted the new burgesses as they entered and took their seats.

Andros could feel a wave of support and friendship from the newly assembled body. He knew many of them personally, and he had the support of most of the sheriffs. They'd seen to it that supporters of the new governor would do well in the elections. William Roscoe, Daniel Parke and Robert Carter won their elections. They would serve as three of forty-eight new member of the House of Burgesses.

After the House was seated and oaths administered, Andros addressed the assembled burgesses.

"Thank you and congratulations on the meeting of this new House of Burgesses. We're here to consider the request of Governor Fletcher of New York for assistance in his war against the French and the Indians. The King has sent specific orders to oblige this request."

Speaker of the House Thomas Milner raised his hand to indicate the beginning of the House debate.

Daniel Parke, burgess from York, struck first. "We've seen the woeful state of our defenses. We'll need to do something about protecting our own frontiers. We also need to discuss the arming of ships, as trade in tobacco is down due to interference by warships at sea."

Thomas Swan of Surry interjected. "But how much can we afford to send to New York, if we have to fit out our own defenses here?"

Several other burgesses joined the discussion. Fear of invasion and new Indian raids spread through the House. There was a full and lively debate and Andros followed the discussion closely.

He finally interjected. "We are obligated to help New York. The French have murdered many Mohawks and threaten to invade the colony. The King wishes that we send New York money. Customs collections are down because the price of tobacco is down. I have requested from the King that I be permitted to take some cash from the quitrents that support the regular administration of Virginia. That won't require special legislation by this House. I've also offered to supplement that with money from my own pocket. I'll loan the colony a thousand pounds forthwith."

The burgesses mumbled in excitement. After some debate, the Speaker moved that the House vote on the question of sending assistance to New York.

The burgesses refused to raise an army to send to New York, as that would have cost them dearly for clothing, armaments and transportation. Andros had previously raised the issue with London, arguing that the main job of the men who'd be sent to New York was to plant tobacco. His new House supported Andros' position. Sending them would cost Virginia and London the value of a good part of the tobacco crop.

The House ended the session by raising a thousand pounds for the war. Several members spoke of Andros' offer to pay for it. The Speaker of the House said, "These are monies for our defense, and will be raised from the people who live here. We appreciate the Governor's offer, but he is sent from London to do the King's bidding. He receives a salary and should keep it."

Andros, though he made the offer, didn't have to pay from his own pocket. He knew he'd increased respect for his views by the burgesses, and he now counted many of them as personal friends.

The session ended abruptly, as many members felt the need to return to their homes to begin the spring planting. William Roscoe was among them. He'd made a number of friends from outlying counties, and while he supported the Governor, he was sincere in his vote to send money and not troops. If he were to send troops, his friends in the militia would have to go, and they really were just farmers and fishermen.

<hr />

William, after his return from Charles Towne, brought his wares to Archie Blair, who was delighted with the Carolina clothing. When he saw the ladies' dresses, he exclaimed, "These are as beautiful as any I've been able to get from England. The men's coats also have a fine cut to them. Our people here will love them, and I know several ladies who have maids to do proper alterations."

William also visited Mrs. Custis, bringing her packages and several letters from her French relatives. She was happy to see him as well. "How did your journey go? Are you in business now?"

"I've managed to sell a shipload, which Captain Crowe exchanged for rice. He's taking it to Holland, says he makes three trips a year."

"Crowe? I thought he was getting rid of the *Revenge*. He's had some close calls at sea with English warships. I understand he likes to shift his flags according to the waters he sails. That's an act of piracy, if you're caught."

She smiled at William, "As they say, nothing ventured, nothing gained. Welcome to the real world of commerce, William. You might find you'd rather be a sheriff. Crowe is a very rich man for his efforts."

William always enjoyed talking to Mrs. Custis. "Thanks to the Du Boises and Bardons, I've met most of the merchants in Charles Towne. I think I can keep up an inland trade for small manufactures. We need to do more here, but poor Jamestown is such a backwater. I think perhaps we should get serious about building a new capital city."

"King William has to finish his war first, I think. Does the Governor support the idea? I know many of the large planters would like a real capital, with streets and shops."

"He cares mostly for defense, but we'll have a full debate when the burgesses meet."

"Well, I wish you success. Remember to tell me if I can be of assistance. I want you to remain a burgess."

William next visited the Wests. They held their annual picnic the second week William was back, and William wanted to speak to his fellow burgess, Thomas West. This year the West picnic was a sort of business meeting for burgesses preparing for the new House session. Daniel Parke spotted William almost as soon as he arrived.

Parke let William get down from his carriage and become situated. He noticed that William had brought some gifts for the host and hostess, and was greeted especially warmly by Rachel West. He overheard her say, "Well, this is a new year. I'm sorry Sarah couldn't make it, as we so enjoyed having you both last year, along with little Jack."

William was being embraced and welcomed to the Wests as if he were a close relative. Parke waited until William came down from his rooms, and when he was alone, he said "Welcome back from Charles Towne. Are you richer or poorer for the trip?"

"Haven't you spoken to your father-in law? I met up with some of your friends there."

"Friends? I know few people in Charles Towne. It's such a busy place; so much going on. I don't know what you mean."

"It's too bad you didn't win the *Revenge* in that card game a while back. It seems Mr. Crowe wanted to collect something from you, and thought he could lift a gun from the *Pretty Polly* to satisfy your debt."

"How foolish of him! Why did he think that?"

"You tell me."

William didn't fear Parke, especially here at the Wests, where he was surrounded by many planters and their families.

Parke instigated. "It's true that I owe him something, but that's just gambling. We have a game scheduled for later in my room. Would you like to join us?"

William felt flush with cash, and he wanted to see some of the other burgesses. "Certainly. I have lots of stories to tell of Charles Towne, and plenty of cash to tell it with."

Parke looked at William. "A ship is a good thing to own, I guess. How did you manage to come into possession of two?"

"A long story, but sometimes a burgess doing his duty can be rewarded."

Parke snickered. "What would it take to buy a piece of one of your ships?"

"Why would you want to do that? You have no interest in business."

"But a ship like the *Good Fortune* as you've equipped her could take our tobacco straight to Holland. We could lower the shipping costs and not share the gains with middlemen and factors here. I know people in Holland who'd buy our good Virginia tobacco at a very good price."

"I'm only part owner of the *Good Fortune*. I can raise the issue with my partner if you like."

"Why don't you do it sooner? It's already October, and the crop is ready to be shipped as we speak."

"True, Crowe's probably sailed already. I'll talk to Sarah very soon."

William went up to the card game, but stayed only a short while. He noticed Parke was losing one large sum after another. William had ideas for fixing his ships and improving his plantation for the cash he had, and left the game with very small winnings.

The following week William met Sarah at the pier in Yorktown. They hadn't seen each other for two weeks, since he'd sailed to Charles Towne. They were overjoyed to be together again, and embraced when they saw each other.

"How well you look," Sarah said. "I understand from George that you were treated very well by our new French friends and Lady Frances. I saw Andrew, and he's healing well. I have him helping on the *Good Fortune*."

William laughed. "I'll tell you everything." And he proceeded to relate a fully embellished story of the pirates, the meeting with Crowe, and his sale of the tobacco.

William then said, "This all began with Daniel and his debts. Crowe though he could collect some of them from me. I just spoke with Daniel last week. He says he'd like to buy a piece of the *Good Fortune*. He sees it crossing the Atlantic from here, all the way to Europe, without factors and middlemen."

"But William, that's exactly what we should do. I've already loaded a good bit of my tobacco and part of my brother's crop for a trip to Holland. I know the Dutch factors myself. We don't need another partner. Especially Daniel: he's in so much debt, he could never pay for a piece of the *Good Fortune*."

"Shall I tell him you don't agree?"

"Don't say that there's no way. In business, you always have a deal or a price in mind. Let me talk to Jane. She knows how much they can afford better than he does."

CHAPTER 14

Daniel Parke had heavy debts, so heavy even he worried about them. Every time he came home from playing cards, his wife asked about the outcome. His creditors were coming to Jane. After all, she was a Ludwell and step-daughter to Lady Frances. Everyone in Jamestown knew she ran the extensive Parke plantation.

One evening, Jane said to Daniel, "Can you just stop gambling for a while? We're at war. We can't settle your debts by burning bricks. We'll soon have to sell off the land. Do you want us all to end up paupers?"

Daniel never abused Jane when they were alone together. "I have to keep up appearances, Jane. I'm aide to the Governor and a burgess. I'm also a colonel in the militia. I have to see people to play cards, just to keep abreast of local opinion. That's what I report to the Governor."

"But Daniel, do you always have to lose so much? Can't you

moderate your habits some way?"

He shrugged his shoulders, but could figure no way out of it. He was no businessman, but he knew that the people with money owned ships. The ships went down to the Caribbean, and were armed to seize or be seized. The cargoes they brought back were sold at very high prices. Daniel wanted to get into this action. "What if I could get a price on a ship? Would we have money for that?"

"What kind of ship?" Jane asked. "I hope you don't mean to make a deal with outright pirates."

"No, no. You know that William Roscoe and Sarah Blair own the *Good Fortune*. Do you ever talk to Sarah about her business?"

A few years older than Sarah Blair, Jane was lifelong friends with her. Both had grown up with attentive mothers active in business affairs, and both had rich, powerful, political fathers. When they were girls, they spent many hours discussing the things young girls talked about: clothes, parties, men and the future. Both were well-educated: they could read and keep accounts. Both could run plantations or other businesses. Jane married Daniel Parke in 1685; Sarah married James Blair in 1687. The women remained close friends, and they knew a great deal about each other's business.

"We talk about lots of things. I knew she and William owned the ship, but she hasn't mentioned to me where it has gone and what its cargo has been."

"Could you find out?"

"I'll see her this Sunday. She and her mother have been using the pew in church in Jamestown. I could go there and see if I can find out anything."

"I'll be going to Bruton Parish in Middle Plantation. See what you can find out," Parke said.

Parke was in deep debt to Crowe, and had heard that William had struck up some regular deal with him. He was trading tobacco for rice, and going back and forth from Charles Towne in the *Pretty Polly*, but Parke knew the *Good Fortune* had previously been up and down the seaboard to the Caribbean.

The next day when both Parke and William were waiting to see the Governor in the Governor's offices, Parke said to William, "How's the shipping business? I hear you have a nice arrangement with Crowe?"

William didn't mind Parke asking, but didn't know what to say. "Yes, I have the *Pretty Polly* going down twice a year. The cargo back from Charles Towne is always desired here. We get very high prices for the deerskins and the clothing."

"Are you going soon? I might have some tobacco to load, if you have the room."

"We leave in three weeks. I think we have the space. Let me see about it, and I'll let you know in a few days. Do you know where our pier is, on the York?"

"Yes I know, and thank you. What about your other ship, the *Good Fortune*? It used to be a regular down to the Caribbean and back."

"We've got her properly equipped with guns, and an experienced crew. But we haven't yet spoken to factors."

"If you went down to the Caribbean, you won't need factors. Privateers can cut out middlemen and keep a lot more of the profits for themselves."

"I'm not sole owner of the *Good Fortune*. We're still discussing whether to go down south, or try to run the warships and get to Amsterdam. Sarah is well acquainted with the Dutch factors and thinks we can do really well, by just sticking to tobacco. So little gets through now, that a loaded tobacco ship can hope to do very well in the European market."

"But the Caribbean is so much closer. Can I invest with you in a shipment to the Caribbean? I can help you find a proper captain and crew."

"You know, Daniel, I'd love to have you as a partner, but this isn't for me to negotiate on my own."

"Think about it. Jane may talk to Sarah this Sunday. Perhaps you both can come to dinner one day next week."

William slapped Parke on the back, and said, "That would be fine with me. I'll talk to Sarah. Don't worry too much, Daniel. Business has to pick up one of these days. People need their tobacco."

⁘

The following Sunday, Jane and Sarah sat next to each other in Philip Ludwell's pew in the Jamestown church. Jane had mentioned Daniel's interest in the *Good Fortune*, and Sarah asked, "Why is he so interested so suddenly?"

"I fear it has something to do with his gambling debts or card partners. I don't know who these people are, to tell you the truth."

"Is it wise or even safe to do business with them?'

"I couldn't tell you. To tell the truth, I worry about the people he has dealings with. He hasn't gone a year since he's back without some fight or some duel, almost always over money.

How are things with you, Sarah? Are you still seeing William?"

"Yes, we both go up to the York from time to time to look over the two boats. William is only half owner of the *Good Fortune*, a faster, more heavily armed ship. He's a sweet fellow, and has a regular business on the *Pretty Polly* with Charles Towne now. He knows the makers of clothes and the retailers, and has a deal with the warehousemen. You must know. He stops to see Lady Frances every time he goes down there. I'm afraid he's very honest, and willing to wait until things roll his way in business. He loves the camaraderie, but isn't one for taking great risks."

Jane laughed. "That sounds more like you. Have you plans for the *Good Fortune*?"

Sarah smiled. "When McForce ran her, she caught the eye of every warship in the Caribbean. I plan to try an ocean voyage first, a tobacco ship either to England or Holland. I've a new captain and crew, and they are trying to get information together on the best routes. I've also written to the banks and factors. If we get through, it should be a good start on an oceanic business."

"What does William say?

"He goes pale when I talk about it, but he hasn't objected. He leaves the big transactions in my hands."

"What should I tell Daniel?'

"Say, the trip for Europe has been set for now. In a few months we could reassess. Don't be overly encouraging if you're nervous about the people he's been dealing with."

"Yes, I think I'll tell him maybe next year for the Caribbean. Would that be all right?"

"Who knows where anyone will be next year?"

The following week, Jane and Daniel had a long talk. "Daniel, you can't just expect everyone to jump to attention just because you've got a new business idea. Running cargo ships is a risky venture. Ships have to deal with the weather and war. The English, Dutch and French all have warships on the ocean and in the Caribbean."

Parke raised his voice in irritation. "But a ship from the Caribbean can charge a fortune for the cargo it brings back!"

"Well, Sarah tells me that the *Good Fortune* is set for Europe, not the Caribbean. Maybe you can try again next year."

Parke didn't say another word, but he was very annoyed. He knew that William had money to burn, but was just salting it away on his two ships and plantation. Parke knew that William was no gambler. He used his cash to buy more land, plant more acres and hire more help. With the help of Sarah Blair, his co-owner of the *Good Fortune*, he was now going to make profits from direct trade with Europe. Parke resented William's new wealth. In less than three weeks William would be back, loaded with Carolina cargo and a fistful of tobacco notes.

On the following Sunday, Daniel Parke visited Jamestown Church. When he entered the building, he heard the minister address the congregation, "We are here today to receive the wisdom of the scriptures. As you all know, we now have a charter to build a college that would educate new ministers of religion. We are thankful for the queen's charter, but we need more support to get the college built. I hope all who can will honor us with contributions. Today's sermon will address the heinous sin of adultery."

Parke didn't go to church looking for a fight, but he was in a state of mind that meant trouble for anyone who annoyed him.

Parke attended church because all Virginians did. But Parke had never liked James Blair, and now he had reason to be resentful of Sarah Blair.

Parke had a general dislike of Virginia clergy, many of whom were from Scotland. Parke thought they were a pack of failures who couldn't succeed in their own country. Parke took a personal dislike to James Blair after the pompous reverend ordered thirty thousand bricks from Parke for construction of the college building, and used the occasion of laying the cornerstone to criticize Governor Andros.

Sarah Blair and Jane Parke had negotiated the purchase, which Jane thought was at a fair price, and Daniel had taken special pains to attend the laying of the cornerstone. Everyone of importance in Jamestown attended, including the Governor, and in the evening there was a great celebration including refreshments and fireworks. At the celebration, Blair complained aloud to all who could hear his scratchy Scottish brogue, "The Governor is here to lay the foundation, but does everything he can to stop the building. He's constantly hiring away workers for other projects." Most people hearing Blair simply laughed. Some shouted, "Are you complaining about laying the foundation? Be happy with what you get, it could be worse!"

Parke, and virtually everyone else at the celebration, knew that Blair referred to defense projects, repairing forts along the rivers. Parke didn't laugh. He couldn't stand the way Blair complained publicly. Parke particularly didn't like to hear people complain about the Governor. Parke thought Governor Andros was a great man.

Parke hadn't attended church when he was away in England, and in his absence, the Ludwell family pew in Jamestown was regularly occupied by Sarah Blair. Parke knew that Sarah often attended the church with his wife, Jane. When he entered the building he saw Sarah sitting quietly in the pew alongside her mother. Jane wasn't there.

He strode over to Sarah and said, "Who told you that you could sit in my pew?"

"I've been coming for almost two years, with the kind permission of my landlord, Mr. Philip Ludwell, your father-in law." Sarah was renting the Blair plantation from the Ludwells.

Sarah was expensively dressed in a dark red velvet gown. Though the wife of a clergyman, she retained the aura and status of a member of the Harrison family, among the wealthiest in Virginia. The Harrisons and the Parkes were equal socially, knew with each other very well, and Daniel knew that Sarah was a good friend of his wife. But Parke was angry at Blair and Sarah, and the sight of Sarah in her expensive clothes, sitting in his pew, made him even angrier.

Parke shouted. "This is my pew, and I've given no permission for its use by anyone." With that he grabbed Sarah by the wrist and pulled her physically out of the pew. This caused a great commotion in the church. People stood and murmured, and hurried to get out of Parke's way. Many hurried their families out of the building.

Minister Eberne saw the whole incident and pleaded, "Please relent, sir. Nobody has done you harm."

Parke responded. "You've allowed my pew to be occupied without my permission. That's theft, and I don't tolerate theft. I intend to get my sword."

Minister Eberne, nearly in tears, begged, "Against whom would you use a sword, today, on Sunday? Would you murder the minister's wife? Please forgive us. I had nothing to do with this."

Parke strode to the front of the church while Sarah and her mother, and many other people who were in the back of the church, left the building quietly. He stood erect facing Eberne, a short plump man. The minister knew that Daniel Parke was a fine swordsman with a hot temper. Though Parke was not armed in the church, he might have kept a horse and weapons nearby.

The minister paled and his hands were shaking. "Sir, I've done no wrong here. I fear your anger, and for that reason I resign this post, here and now. I'll return to England as soon as I can find passage."

Eberne had no chance at self-defense, and he'd been witness to the norms of Virginians, decidedly different than in England. In Virginia, families saw to their own defense. Many people carried muskets or pistols or brandished swords. Duels were commonplace, and pretty much every young man was skilled in the combat arts. They had to be skilled to survive, and many didn't. Eberne couldn't get away from Virginia quickly enough.

Parke goaded the impish minister. "Well, probably London is safer for you. You'll find many more coats to hide behind when you utter your blasphemous charges."

The following week, Reverend Blair brought the incident of Parke's behavior toward his wife and the church minister to the attention of Governor Andros. The Governor would have no part in the dispute. He thought James Blair couldn't separate his personal and family disputes from the Governor's business, and Blair was now off the council anyway. All he said was, "The issue doesn't lie before me."

CHAPTER 15

The world was at war. Virginia was suffering economically and in military danger, and few people in the colony understood the situation better than Lady Frances Berkeley, the wife of Philip Ludwell. In 1694, she and her husband, the Governor of Carolina, moved back to Virginia. Philip became Speaker of the House of Burgesses, and Lady Frances was able to see her step-children and grandchildren and follow a much more active social and political life. She came back to support the Governor, something Lady Berkeley always did when it was in the interests of Virginia. Times were dangerous. and she felt it was time to look to the interests of the colony.

Lady Berkeley was born in England in 1634 when her father, Thomas Culpeper, owned shares in the Virginia Company of London. Thomas Culpeper brought his family of three sons and two daughters to Virginia in 1650, at the height of the English civil wars. Cromwell was dictator and religious warfare raged.

Frances, then sixteen years old, was Thomas Culpeper's youngest child. Under English law, landowners could add fifty acres to their estate for every indentured servant brought over. Using the rules of English law, Culpeper added to his estate, and when he arrived in Virginia, he owned thousands of acres, including the entire Northern Neck between the Potomac and Rappahannock Rivers. Lady Frances represented a powerful family in Virginia, and three years later she married Captain Samuel Stephens, Governor of the Albemarle Settlements in Carolina.

When Governor Stephens died in 1669, his widow inherited his estate of well over a thousand acres. Under Virginia law, as a widow with no children she was the absolute owner of the Stephens property, along with property given to her by her father as a dowry when she was married. When she married Governor Sir William Berkeley of Virginia in 1670, she was one of the largest landowners in North America.

Lady Frances grew to adulthood in Virginia. She was wealthy, well-educated, and could run a large plantation. She also understood the practice of politics. Everyone in Virginia knew that it was Lady Berkeley who'd convinced the king to send a thousand troops to put down Bacon's Rebellion in 1677. She'd spent her life as a consort to royal governors sent to Virginia by the King.

Lady Frances kept a constant correspondence with relatives and friends in England, including people in high positions at the royal court. She visited England frequently. But Lady Frances Berkeley saw herself as a Virginian, and never considered moving back to the mother country, something that men who met hard times in Virginia occasionally did. Her wealth, her family and her future interests were all tied to Virginia, and she was a person who planned ahead, who cared about her future, and about the future of her children.

⟨ornament⟩

In 1695, Lady Frances was sixty-two years old and not feeling very strong or healthy. A contemporary to Governor Andros, she shared childhood memories similar to his. Both remembered the horrors of England's religious civil wars. She felt a certain kinship with him because of that, and now decided to speak with him directly.

She took a carriage from the Ludwell plantation into Jamestown to see Andros. Philip was at the House of Burgesses, and Parke was out playing cards with gambling friends. She decided not to tell Jane about this visit.

When arriving at the Governor's offices, she was quickly recognized and announced. She didn't need an appointment or invitation: the Governor immediately made time for her, considering her a good friend. "Welcome back to Jamestown! Would you like a cup of tea?"

She thanked him and quickly sat. It was hot, and she feared a flare-up of malaria coming on. Andros also had a touch of the illness, and he understood completely.

"Sir Edmund, you've heard about Daniel's latest silliness? He pulled Mrs. Blair out of our family pew, and made a public fuss over nothing." Lady Frances inquired.

"Yes," said Andros. "Blair's already been here to complain about it, but I told him that private matters are private. The Governor's business is for the colony."

"Thank you, but there is more to worry about than Blair.

Daniel Parke has large debts, and I fear he's acting in a way to endanger himself. I know he plays with louts and pirates, and I fear he's bitten off more than he can chew. He's killed two people in duels just this year. As you know, people in this colony can be very serious about collecting debts. Some of them might get a gang together, and there's no use asking for a duel then. You've been a wonderful protector, but we worry for his family as well."

"He's a very brave and strong boy, and a fine assistant. But I know your meaning. Strange that both of us have no children of our own, but concern ourselves about family more so than many with natural offspring. I worry about my own stepson sometimes."

"You must understand. It's not the money; we can deal with his debts, if his behavior would change. But he's gotten into a life here where there's no end in sight, and I'm afraid he takes advantage of being your assistant. He sees himself as part of the government. It makes his gambling grander than it needs to be. Daniel will never let anyone outbid him on any matter."

"He's very good at what he does for me. He understands the military needs of the colony and he's quick to volunteer his time. He's gone on a few missions by himself, and returned with fine reports."

"Yes, but I worry about my grandchildren and the prospects for Lucy and Frances. They can hardly find proper husbands if their father is a rake and leaves them nothing but debts. I worry for their future."

"We need to think of all our futures."

Andros looked wistful. He thought of Europe and the wars unfolding there. While the war in North America consisted of French and Indian raids of English colonies along the frontiers and the northern borders, Andros knew that the war was global, not local. He had friends fighting for the King on the continent. and he worried for his relatives and home in Guernsey, just a few miles off the coast of France.

Andros exchanged letters frequently with friends in the military. He knew that the European war was extensive and very bloody. Generals and heroes were being made, while many young soldiers were losing their lives. Thousands of civilians were also dying all over Europe. The issues of religion, free trade on the seas, the ambitions of Louis XIV, and the status of James II, who was still alive and living in France, roiled the politics of Europe.

"I have friends in England. I could write to see if Daniel could be placed as an aide to a military personage there. Do you think that would help?" Andros offered.

Lady Frances smiled. "How well we understand each other. That would likely save Daniel's life, as I think he won't last much longer in Virginia. Jane can handle the plantation, but his debts are enormous and his gambling partners very dangerous. I can't thank you enough for your kindness. After all, what are we, if we don't see to the benefit of the children?"

"How strange that war will be Daniel's savior, while it is the death and worry of everyone else."

"Not strange at all. He's played at soldier all his life, and we have no standing army here. Everyone in the militia is a colonel. Daniel doesn't take well to being equal to anyone. Without you, my Governor, he has nobody to look up to. He loves the idea of being attached to a King's representative. There can be no greater royalist than Daniel."

"I enjoy having him near me and will have no problem

supporting him to my friends. But I find it strange that he has no use for other community leaders. Look how he insults Commissary Blair. It can do him no good. He doesn't realize that people remember insults."

"I know. He sees himself as a royalist, a sort of knight on horseback. You are the royal person here, so you have all of his support. All other people in the community, for Daniel, rank below you, in a sort of hierarchy. He sees Commissary Blair as a foreigner and the church as nothing more than an organization of trouble-makers. He's no philosopher."

"I'm no philosopher either, but we both know that the only way to stop a war is to negotiate a peace. That takes a little mutual respect, observation of the diplomatic rules, and willingness to bargain. Daniel's been a burgess. I'm surprised you say he doesn't understand that."

"Daniel doesn't bargain. He's never had a high opinion of his role as burgess."

"But the burgesses here really do have the support of the people. If I could tell you what it was like in New England, you wouldn't believe the differences."

Lady Berkeley laughed. "Yes, we hear all sorts of strange stories about people in the north. Did they give you trouble?"

"I had little difficulty in New York. I was the first governor after the Dutch handed over New Amsterdam. I got along well with the assembly there, and even reached a treaty with the five Indian nations. When I became Governor of the Dominion of New England, assemblies became difficult to deal with. They wanted to meet so often, I would have spent all my time going from assembly to assembly.

"You must know that Massachusetts is full of religious

fanatics. A governor has to think of the whole colony, its defenses and its economy. Religion is fine, but not what the King sent me there to preside over." Andros shook his head, "Of course, the King was overthrown in 1689, and that ended the dominion. Massachusetts is Massachusetts again; good thing for everybody."

Lady Frances sipped her tea. "I appreciate your idea of a military position for Daniel in Europe. It would be a simpler life for him. He simply cannot respect more than one master. He has scant respect for law, courts, church, and even his family. It's as if he never grew out of playing at duels and combat. He makes a fine military assistant, but he needs to be part of a battle to be really happy."

Andros thought a bit. He felt nothing but respect and a little affection for Lady Frances. "My friend John Churchill will soon lead a large military force on the continent. He'll be right in the thick of things."

"I believe I met him and his charming wife the last time I was in England. She's good friends with Princess Anne, isn't she?"

"Yes, they've been friends for years. Anne is next in line for the throne, as William and Mary had no children. We are in quite a state, aren't we? Our Kings and Queens fight over territory and religion, stopping all commerce for everyone. Soldiers kill each other and civilians if they're in the way, but never resolve the problem. The only time people talk to each other is between battles."

Lady Frances laughed. "Yes, they could learn something from Virginia and the Indians. After a lot of bloodshed, we finally learned that any treaty is better than any war, and that farming and commerce are worth more to the people living here than an army or navy. We've given up royal pomp and soldiers marching, though the people love to see the red tunics and the great fireworks."

Andros was gracious. "I'll write to Churchill right away. I'm sure everything will work out for Daniel."

Lady Frances smiled but she wasn't feeling well. She put down her teacup, and stood. She said, "Thank you, Governor. I've enjoyed our talk and trust in you."

Two weeks later, Lady Frances was dead.

CHAPTER 16

William Byrd II was born in Virginia in 1674. His father, the son of a London goldsmith, came to Virginia at the invitation of an uncle and inherited the uncle's estate. William Byrd I owned and accumulated property, became wealthy planting tobacco, was a leader in Virginia society and joined the House of Burgesses.

When young William was two years old, his parents sent him back to England for fear of the dangers of Bacon's rebellion. He stayed there for his education. He attended the Felsted Grammar School in Essex and, when he was fifteen, went to Holland as an apprentice to his father's business agent. There he learned about trade and tobacco commerce. In 1690, William returned to England to study law at the Honourable Society of the Middle Temple, and was admitted to the bar in London. He was present in England when party politics began in the Parliament after the removal of King James II in 1689.

Young Byrd, though only nineteen years old, was appointed
agent for the Virginia House of Burgesses, where he represented
the interests of the colony before England's Board of Trade.
After failing to get an appointment to the Board, Byrd decided
to return home to Virginia.

When Byrd arrived, his parents were delighted and held a
great celebration. The Harrisons, Parkes, Ludwells, Carters,
Lees, and Custises all were in attendance. William was delighted
to meet the numerous young ladies. He impressed the older men
with his knowledge and very English speech. He impressed the
ladies with his polish and dancing.

He approached the Governor, "Sir, I'm delighted to finally
be in Virginia. I've been speaking for the colony in the Board of
Trade these last two years."

Andros, amused, shook his hand and said, "We are delighted
to have you here. You must tell us about the Board of Trade and
the Parliament."

Byrd smiled as a number of the members of the Governor's
Council gathered around. "Well, the Board is today dominated
by people not well disposed to Virginia. Mr. John Locke, who
wrote of the rights of all to life, liberty and property, is a member.
He's most concerned about property, and would like to get his
hands on as much of ours as possible. He would undermine the
security of the colonies if it enriched him."

"Well, what should we do about it?"

"We must have someone there to represent us," Byrd said. "
I plan to return next year. It's a time of warfare and the King and
his ministers are distracted by the military conflict with France.
But tell me, what is new here in Virginia?"

A number of people gathered to answer. "We've rebuilt the

state house."

"We've fortified the frontiers against the Indians from the North."

"We've laid the cornerstone for a new college in Middle Plantation."

This caught Byrd's interest. "Tell me about the college. This will be wonderful for the future."

"The Reverend Blair brought back a charter for a college signed by Queen Mary, and we've begun with the building, although its going slowly as there is little money for it. There's a temporary building housing a small grammar school with a few instructors. Governor Nicholson of Maryland gave the money for that."

"Who governs the college?" Byrd asked. "Who decides what's to be taught?"

"Why, the Reverend Blair, of course," Governor Andros said with a smirk. "He had himself appointed president of the college when he brought back the charter. Nicholson agreed to it. There's also a Board of Trustees that's made some contributions. The King has asked that quitrents not be spent on the college, and has promised to revisit his decision in three years. Blair is receiving an annual payment from the quitrents as salary as President."

"How does he receive a salary as an officer of the college when the college is not yet built?" Byrd asked.

Robert Carter, standing nearby, said "Yes. He tried to sue several of us for our subscriptions, but times are harsh. When the King held back the quitrents for defense, we felt we'd wait also. Blair simply demanded his salary from the treasurer based on documents he brought back from London."

Byrd responded, "That seems inappropriate. The public monies shouldn't be paid for services that aren't being rendered. If there is no college, its president shouldn't be collecting a salary. That's my humble legal opinion."

The council members and Governor looked at each other. The next week the Governor ordered that Blair not receive a salary to run a nonexistent college.

In early 1695, Andros appointed Daniel Parke to the Council. This raised Daniel's profile in the community and helped him hold off some of his creditors. The Governor followed the war in Europe closely, corresponding with friends in the government and the military. He hoped to see an end to the dire economic circumstances facing the colony. Virtually anything not related to defense couldn't be supported with the threats of France high and tobacco income low.

After Blair had been asked by the Council to leave, Andros wrote the Commissioners on the Board of Trade telling them of the ouster. At the same time, Blair wrote to friends in London asking for advice on what to do about finding financial support for the college.

When Andros didn't hear back from the Board of Trade confirming Blair's ouster, he restored Blair to the Council in 1696. That move was punctuated when the Parliament declared that only native-born subjects of England could hold positions of "trust" in the colony. Upon receiving the declaration, Andros immediately called a meeting of his council to consider the matter.

Once the council convened, Blair insisted on speaking. He

stood, walked around the impressive table, and said, "I know you think of me as a foreigner—a Scots hireling. I am a native of Scotland, but I am here for the Church of England to which I have given my life. I hold the seat dedicated to the Commissary of the Church."

General debate and discussion began, with the members finally asking Andros what the rules were. What was the English law?

"According to the Board of Trade's last correspondence, all places of trust—that would include the courts, the House of Burgesses, this council, and likely our militia—must be in the hands of native-born subjects of England. I interpret that to mean that anyone born in the Dominion of Virginia is native born and may hold such seats. Foreigners may not. Scotland is not England; it is a foreign country, though I'm uncertain of the status of the church commissary. As for me, I believe we should wait before excluding Commissary Blair."

Blair challenged Andros. "Does that mean you'd bar the Commissary of the Church from sitting in the general court or council, when considering the use of colonial moneys?"

Andros responded, trying very hard not to be angry with the determined preacher. "I haven't said we should exclude you. I believe the Commissary should have a seat on the Council, and we should wait to have the Board of Trade clarify your status."

The Council considered the matter and asked Blair to absent himself until his status could be clarified. The Council, led by Daniel Parke but following the Act of Parliament, wanted Blair off. Andros said nothing. The Council meeting ended as Blair stood up and announced, "These proceedings are insulting. I will go to London to see about how the Board truly feels on these matters."

Blair understood English law and politics, and obviously this hadn't helped him in Virginia. Blair knew the factions in the English Parliament, and generally supported the Whigs who wanted to limit the king. Since governors were royal appointees, Blair reasoned that the Board of Trade would wish to limit the power of governors. He thought that Board of Trade members simply wanted to enrich themselves personally from business with the colonies, having little interest in actual colonial life. After all, Blair lived there and had little knowledge or understanding of Virginia as well.

On the other hand, Blair knew that the Board of Trade couldn't restrain a royal appointee so long as the King was at war. And wars were permanent in Europe. When this war lapsed, it would be be superseded by the next one. England's King had a standing army, and aristocrats fought to get into the military and march up its ranks. Countries with standing armies, like England and France, had to keep their soldiers occupied or the armies might become a danger to the home country. Recent European wars were fought in the Low Countries and the German principalities, far away from London and Paris. Death and destruction came to Middle Europeans, not to the English and the French.

Blair regarded the money he raised for the college as his own, to save and spend as he saw fit, and he thought of the college as his personal property. He'd never been opposed in any way until Byrd recommended that Blair not receive a President's salary so long as the college wasn't built. Blair resented Byrd and the Council for that action, though he publicly blamed Andros. While the House of Burgesses and subscriptions had sent him to

London to get the charter five years earlier, he felt no obligation to them. If they didn't support him now, he'd lobby for support elsewhere.

Blair knew that the Governor of Maryland, Francis Nicholson, wanted to be Governor of Virginia. Blair had no particular respect or liking for Nicholson, and still blamed Nicholson for the failure of his proposed ecclesiastical courts. In turn, Nicholson had no particular love for Blair, whom he regarded as narrow-minded and interfering.

Still, Nicholson, now in his thirties, wanted to be out from under the shadow of Sir Edmund Andros. He resented being pushed around and acting as a permanent assistant to someone else. Nicholson was ready to settle down somewhere, but wanted to run a show himself. He was moody and temperamental, and fought everyone he came in contact with. His temper tantrums were known all over Virginia and Maryland.

Nicholson wanted Andros out of Virginia and himself appointed in his place, but personally he wasn't willing to lobby against his old boss. Nicholson, like Andros, was at heart a royalist and opposed to the Whigs on the Board of Trade. He was, however, willing to support James Blair, with lots of money if necessary, to lobby for the college. Education was one of Nicholson's pet projects, and he was willing to spend personal funds promoting it.

Blair and Nicholson met regularly at college trustee meetings and wrote to each other. They reached an understanding. Blair would go back to London to plead for the college, with Nicholson's support.

In the summer of 1697, Blair sailed to London with Nicholson paying his passage. Not long after he arrived, King

William's War ended and the public rejoiced, both in England and Virginia. By the Treaty of Ryswick, England and France agreed to revert to their prewar borders. In North America, the Hudson's Bay Company opposed the peace treaty, which allowed many trading posts to remain in French hands. The war was sure to begin again in a few years, but for the interim, everyone else seemed satisfied. King William appointed a new Board of Trade to govern colonial affairs.

Andros felt relieved after the war ended. Virginia had been stressed financially by the exploits in Europe, but remained intact and, largely, unified. Now over sixty, Andros felt a sense of accomplishment and was ready to retire.

After five years as Governor, Andros suffered the Virginia climate with difficulty. He had occasional bouts with malaria, and took to bed on occasion. His wife Elizabeth hadn't adjusted well to the climate or food, either. Andros also missed London and Guernsey, and his work as Bailiff of Guernsey.

Andros had promised Lady Frances that he would see to the welfare of Daniel Parke. He'd written to his good friend John Churchill. Andros and Churchill had served together in the Yarmouth garrison in London back in the early 1670s. They had both made their careers in the military, and Andros knew Churchill could always use an aide-de-camp. Churchill replied that he'd be happy to take on Parke, and looked forward to receiving him.

Andros was happy that Parke would be settled in England, far away from creditors and persons wanting to challenge him to duels for whatever reason. He judged that a military life would be good for Parke, that Parke could use the discipline of being prepared for battle and the experience of dealing with superiors routinely. Andros found Parke to be a diligent assistant and was sure that Churchill would be happy as well.

Parke wasn't so sure. When Andros told him of the appointment, Parke said, "But peace and prosperity are here. Do you think I'd be better off in England?"

"It would be good if you could repair your reputation for your family's sake," Andros said. "You'll have that opportunity in England, but not much opportunity here. I'd take it, Daniel. You'll do well in a military uniform, and Churchill's a good man."

"Well, the Ludwells won't be sorry to see me go, though I'll take Julius Caesar and educate him in England. Jane is always complaining about the debts. She should be used to that by now," Parke said.

"Daniel, you have a family. They need you. You should help with the debts if you can," Andros said.

Parke smirked at that and thanked the Governor quietly. He'd once lived in England and felt safe to go back. He was looking forward to meeting Churchill already. "Thank you for your kindness and generosity, Sir Edmund. I'll never forget you, and if you should need me I hope you'll write to me."

"Well, it won't be long till I return to England as well, now that there's peace. Perhaps we can meet back there. We'll keep in touch."

Andros also spoke to William Byrd II, who impressed him as an able young fellow with a good legal mind. Byrd decided to return to London where he again would be the official agent for Virginia before the Parliament and the Board of Trade. Parke and Byrd were both relatively young men—Parke was twenty-eight and Byrd was twenty-three. Andros thought they could be good friends, and he suggested that they travel to London together.

Parke and Byrd remained in Jamestown to celebrate the wedding of Hannah Harrison to Philip Ludwell II. Hannah was Sarah Blair's younger sister, and Philip the only son of Philip Ludwell, the Speaker of the House of Burgesses. The wedding reception was one of the largest in several years, as money was again flowing from tobacco exports. The Harrisons were doing very well by shipping their tobacco to factors in Scotland.

Sarah took the time to comfort her friend Jane Parke, who still missed her step-mother, Lady Frances. Jane was upset about Daniel going to London, but realized that Daniel wasn't making her life any easier. Every day he amassed new debts from gambling. He'd fought two duels this past year alone. Jane was also irritated with Daniel's mistress, Mrs. Berry, and Mrs. Berry's son, Julius Caesar, and looked forward to being rid of them. The two Parke daughters, now aged nine and eleven, were well aware of their father's behavior, and growing up resentful of their half-brother and men in general. Jane knew Parke would be safer in a country far away, and he likely could take care of himself.

Sarah, happy again now that Blair was away, took the time to wish her younger sister congratulations. She and William were able to see each other more often and more openly. When James was in Virginia, they'd continued their relationship quietly, meeting mostly at the York cottage where the ships were maintained. They still loved each other and William relied on her more than ever, as he was deep into business with Crowe, and commerce was picking up. Warships no longer patrolled the coast, and ships were moving freely.

Sarah also took the time to see Benjamin Harrison IV, now three years old and every family member's favorite. She thought about him often, though not with resentment or remorse. He was her child by birth, but her brother and his wife had loved the boy as their own. The world seemed a happy place, without conflict or confrontation.

⁕

When Blair arrived in London in 1697 he found that the country rejoicing over the end of the war. A new Board of Trade was now dominated by Whigs and presided over by Sir Philip Meadows, a career diplomat who held special responsibility for Virginia and Maryland. Meadows had served as a royal representative and ambassador to several European countries, and was deeply involved in diplomacy with France and Spain. He knew Andros well, having had a long association with other royal Stuart appointees over his career. They were nearly the same age and both had survived the civil wars and the restoration. Sir Philip was the grand old man of the Board of Trade.

The Lord Commissioners of the Board of Trade were wealthy and their positions on the Board of Trade ensured they'd become wealthier. When Blair arrived, their leading intellectual was a Whig, John Locke, the philosopher of the so-called "Glorious Revolution" of 1689 which ended with the deposing of King James II.

Locke wrote about the natural law, and a social contract between government and the governed. This was interpreted to mean that the parliament, especially the House of Commons representing "the people," had the right to hold a King responsible. Locke's Whig Party represented the wealthy non-landed financial interests in England, and Locke himself, though of middle class background, was a wealthy man and investor in overseas projects.

Locke took a personal interest in Blair and invited him to his rooms to discuss Virginia. He and Blair had certain backgrounds in common. Both were born into the educated non-titled classes. Locke's father was a lawyer; Blair's a clergyman. Locke was a trained physician; Blair an educated Anglican minister.

Locke, as member of the Board of Trade, received a large salary and held shares in the Royal African Company, which sold slaves to the colonies. He'd drafted the constitution of Carolina, which established a system of slavery governed by a feudal aristocracy, where masters exercised absolute power. The slaves, of course, would be purchased from the Royal African Company, in which Locke had personal investments. Locke was very interested in Virginia, the largest and most profitable colony in North America.

Blair entered his town house in central London late in the afternoon. Locke had his servants serve tea, and both men sat comfortably by the fire in Locke's grand parlor. Locke's home was full of French furniture, Persian carpets, gilded mirrors, and Italian paintings. He asked Blair to tell him about Virginia.

Blair was no philosopher and knew relatively little about the Virginia plantations, even though he lived on one. Slavery existed in Virginia, but in Jamestown the institution hadn't become widespread. Virginia's laboring classes consisted mostly of indentured servants who worked under contracts. Indentured servants were mostly young English men who accepted a contract for seven years' labor in exchange for their passage.

For the seven years they belonged to their employers, much like slaves who were purchased without labor contracts.

"Poor Virginia," Blair said in a condescending tone. "The land has extraordinary natural advantages: fertile soil, great navigable rivers and creeks, an open coast on the sea all year long. It has easy access to fresh water and plenty of fish, fowl and wild beasts. The place has great forests, minerals, vines and fruits. It has a temperate climate, between extremes of hot and cold. In short, as it came out of the hand of God, it is one of the best countries in the world."

Locke was curious. "Then why are you here? The nature of the place has made it rich. What are the problems?"

Blair continued. "It is a miserable place for people of culture, because when it was founded, no measures were taken to build towns. Most of the governors were against projects from which they made no personal gain. Today people are obstinate about it. They oppose the building of towns, and most members of the assembly in Virginia have never seen a town. They can't imagine the benefits that come from people living in close proximity of each other."

"Possibly they have their reasons. Townhouses and streets are expensive to build, and must come out of the income of the people who'll live there. In the first years, they could hardly have built much, as many died of starvation and fought with the Indians. What are the main industries?"

"The place has possibilities in many industries. There's iron, all kinds of wood, mulberry trees that can produce silk, potash for soap, many grains, including Indian corn, oats, barley, wheat and rice. There's also flax, hemp, cotton. Of course, I would be remiss in not mentioning tobacco. Tobacco has swallowed up everything, to the point that all other crops and industries are neglected. There's so much tobacco, that all markets are virtually glutted with it."

Locke understood the value of tobacco, even if Blair didn't. He knew customs revenues from the purchase and sale of tobacco fed the British treasury. England had fought two wars with Holland over it.

He smiled and said, "Tell me about the people. What are their main pursuits?"

Blair thought a moment. He had so little experience with most Virginians. He knew Locke would like a reason to promote slavery, but he couldn't figure a way to get that into his description.

"Well, there are three main groups: planters, tradesmen, and merchants. Planters are the most numerous, but much of the land is not yet cleared. When tobacco wears out the land, planters simply expand into the fields and woods. Tobacco drives the expansion of the colony; tobacco brings more money into the colony than anything else, and the Virginians see money as the answer to all things. Since there are no towns or markets and hardly any cash, there is little encouragement for tradesmen and artificers. Everything runs on tobacco and tobacco notes. A tradesman can't buy food and other things in a market as we do in London. He has to ride around the country to find corn and meat to buy. He has to spend much time visiting the plantations where most of the work is done. Because the costs to tradesmen are so high, they must charge very high prices for their work. They have a very difficult life."

"What about merchants?"

"They live well, but suffer many inconveniences because

there are no towns and town centers. Because everything is driven by tobacco, all boats load tobacco first. All purchases and sales are in the form of tobacco notes. Merchants have to wait until tobacco is loaded and unloaded before they can get their hands on the goods. They have to figure a way to get their freight from the waterfront, usually a great distance from the plantations where most people live. Goods probably cost double what they should, due to a lack of way of delivering goods to people."

"Why do you think they continue this way? If it's costly to them, they must know it."

"They are an obstinate people. If they make their money off tobacco, they are pleased to spend it through the factors who buy the tobacco from them. Their tobacco is sold all over Europe. The great planters are rich; their houses are full of European furnishings. If it costs them a little more, they have the money to pay for it. There's no starvation in Virginia now."

"So they have trade, mainly in tobacco, but no banks and no cash currency. Is that what you think the main problems are?"

"The Governor and the House of Burgesses are against money dealings. They think it's cheaper to use their quitrents. Tobacco is their currency. There's little need for cash in the system they've established, and they worry that new coins may not use the right amount of metal. They especially worry about bad silver. During the last assembly, the House of Burgesses sent up a bill for ascertaining all coin. It was thrown out in the Governor's Council without any discussion or amendments. There's no standard for coinage anywhere in North America. The Virginians have more trust in their tobacco."

"Do you have anything else to say about the planters?"

"Just that the king's land was given away early on in such a way that the place simply isn't well-peopled. The land was given away in fifty- and hundred-acre lots to encourage adventurers to come. The adventurers stayed and became the planters; the land remaining in the King's hands is worthless, producing no quitrents. There is no way to encourage the building of towns and townships now."

"Tell me about the government. I understand you have great concern about how we govern the colony."

"Well, we have had a revolution here, but in Virginia all of the great offices are heaped on one man, the Governor. I'll list his powers for you: he represents the King in all things. He grants lands, names officers in places of trust in the government, calls and dissolves their assemblies, denies or agrees to their laws, and he decides between peace and war. He's His Majesty's Lieutenant-General and Commander-in-Chief, and raises and commands all militia and land forces. He builds or demolishes all fortifications. As Vice-Admiral of Virginia's Seas, he commands all ships and seamen, lays on and takes off all embargoes and takes account of all prizes. As Lord Treasurer, he issues warrants for paying out all public moneys. As Lord Chancellor, he decides all cases in chancery. As Lord Chief Justice, he sits in all cases that dispose of life, liberty and property. As Bishop, he grants all marriage licenses, inducts ministers and decides all ecclesiastical causes."

"But we do this in all our plantations. The Governor is the King in the plantation where he presides. He reports to our Board of Trade. If the colony is peaceful and profitable, we deem he's doing his job. If he has the support of his council and the House of Burgesses, we think he's keeping his people happy."

"But there are no checks on the Governor. He and his council can do as they like without anyone knowing what they are doing. There is no way of knowing what London instructs them to do. Also, he can remove anyone who disagrees with him from his council. He has great influence with the House of Burgesses by naming officers, such as judges, county clerks, and customs officers in each of the counties. Many burgesses are beholden to the Governor for the livelihood of themselves and their relatives."

"Well, we're really no different. It's better to put someone you know in office than some stranger."

"The House of Burgesses is a confused place. The laws are neither of England nor of Virginia. The laws seem to serve the current whims of people who care little for consistency."

"I understand that Governor Andros has taken great pains to review the laws of Virginia, and is currently bringing them into consistency. It's a big job, apparently, and of course courts in Virginia have their own precedents. Circumstances affect the law as well as the written word; judges and courts have to serve their people."

"I'd like to mention the college we're building..."

Blair rambled on about building the college, his efforts and how he was ultimately thwarted. Locke could tell the reverend felt jilted. His tone had turned from conversational to adversarial. Blair ended his diatribe. "Perhaps now that the war is over, the King can reconsider the matter of funding the college."

Locke suggested, "Why don't you prepare a report for the Board of Trade? Tell us about the land, the people, the government and, if you like, the church and the college. I'm sure the Board will be very interested in all you have to say."

Blair was delighted. Virginia would be seen though his eyes, strengthening the case for his agenda. He would finally be able to exact revenge on Governor Andros.

CHAPTER 17

The Board of Trade in 1697 had a strong majority of Whig members. Of the eight sitting members, seven were Whigs. They wanted to apply their principles of limiting executive power to the governors of the colonies. This coincided in one sense with the principle that the parliament in England should limit the English monarch. On the other hand, limiting the power of colonial governors was the same as limiting the rights of the colonies altogether. It meant that the Board of Trade would govern the colonies, regardless of their established executive, legislative and judicial authorities. Limiting Andros was the same as limiting Virginia's House of Burgesses and Virginia's Governor's Council.

The Board consisted of wealthy investors, and they favored policies that would make themselves wealthier. If the Board's policies harmed the people in the colonies, that didn't bother these silken Whigs. They weren't administrators. They'd never visited the colonies and felt no responsibility to the people living there.

Blair's memorial described in blunt detail how much contempt he felt for Virginia, its people and its Governor. He explained in petty detail every charge he could imagine to criticize Andros. He began by stating that Andros mistreated the clergy, and was unconcerned about empty parishes. He accused Andros of refusing to raise the stipends of clergy as ordered by the king. Blair argued that he personally should have received a greater salary as a member of the clergy.

Blair accused Andros of fomenting against the ecclesiastical power of the Bishop of London.

⁂

Blair's marriage to Sarah Harrison, and his life among the wealthiest of Virginians because of it, was well known to William Blathwayt and the other members of the Board. Blair's report, they knew, was self-serving and exaggerated. It was an outright denunciation of the Governor, a vendetta filled with inflammatory statements of corruption and even treason. Blair was obviously a man scorned and angry for not having his way with the colonists.

Andros was well known to most members of the Board of Trade. Although he might not have been a political ally of theirs, the Virginia Governor had a reputation as an upstanding, loyal servant to the crown. Board members were well aware of the King's orders to Andros to support King William's War in New York. They also were well aware of Andros' record in military matters and fortifications.

The Board was appointed by King William, Andros'

childhood friend. Philip Meadows, another friend of Andros and fellow military leader, presided over it. He knew that the king had relied on Andros for military support, and Andros had provided it.

Blair's memorial ended with a detailed description of petty and personal insults. He described Daniel Parke's confrontation with Nicholson at Blair's home and Parke's ejecting Blair's wife from Parke's pew at church. He related Minister Eberne's resignation from the ministry, and blamed it all on Andros, who Blair described as a friend and supporter of Parke.

The Board of Trade received Blair's memorial, and kept it for a number of weeks. Blair again visited Locke at Locke's home to see what was happening.

Once again they had tea together in the late afternoon. Locke was cordial and asked after Blair's health, as London was dark and smoky with the winter weather moving in.

"I've read your report and memorial. I'm sure many of our board members are very interested in some of the things you have to say."

"Will the board be doing anything? Will you have a proper hearing?"

"I can't say that. We have a full plate, and the board likely won't respond to you directly on the report. We generally don't take actions on the basis of written documents. We have procedures for dealing with sitting governors. These are people, as you know, who have great responsibilities."

"What do you recommend I do next?"

"Well, many of your charges involve the church and ecclesiastical matters. Why don't you present yourself to the church hierarchy here in London? They could hold a hearing at Lambeth. I'm sure if you contact the Bishop of London he can get the Archbishop of Canterbury to chair the hearing. The Board of Trade doesn't deal with ecclesiastical matters."

This was a bureaucratic response to a bureaucrat who understood what he was being told. The Board of Trade dealt with the colonies, but arguments about the church had to go through the church. The Board of Trade would do nothing about a governor without a formal public hearing where the Governor was represented. It would all involve a lot of legal documents and lawyers' arguments. Blair understood the law and bureaucracy well. The very next day he visited Henry Compton to see about setting up a church hearing.

On December 27, 1697, James Blair, Commissary of the Church of England in Virginia, presented charges against Sir Edmund Andros at a hearing before a three-judge panel at Lambeth Palace, the headquarters of the Anglican Church in London. Blair stood in a cavernous hearing room, paneled in dark wood, decorated floor to ceiling with religious artworks. The room held seats for a few dozen spectators, but these were mostly empty. Thomas Tenison, the Archbishop of Canterbury, presided over the hearing.

The other two judges were Henry Compton, the Bishop of London, who'd sent Blair to Virginia, and John Povey, a clerk of King William's Privy Council. Povey was a tall, thin man in resplendent silk attire, and had read Blair's written report to the Board of Trade and memorial attacking Andros. A week before the hearing, Povey discussed the case with John Locke, and Locke promptly left London for health reasons. Povey had never personally met James Blair, but he knew the members of the Board of Trade very well.

Blair was accompanied by Benjamin Harrison III, his brother-in-law. Harrison had been trained in law at Middle Temple, and at Blair's request came to London from Virginia where he was recently appointed by Andros as Attorney General for the colony.

Harrison felt he wasn't fulfilling his obligations to his family and the colony by being in London. He'd never before been in a London courtroom, and being at an ecclesiastical court hearing was an altogether new experience. Harrison took a chair to the side of the highly decorated room, facing the tall bench that held the three judges. He was prepared to say very little. Blair was ready to do all the talking.

Representing Andros were a London attorney, Ralph Marshall, and William Byrd II. Marshall was a short, plump man with a bellowing voice. He'd known Andros for many years and came to the hearing as requested by Andros family members on Guernsey. Marshall was well-respected in legal circles as a capable family solicitor. He'd drafted and redrafted Andros' will many times, but never to his client's complete satisfaction. He counted Andros as a good friend, and he knew that Andros wouldn't be at this hearing. Marshall and Povey both understood that Andros had responsibilities in Virginia. Colonial governors were not permitted to leave their posts unless ordered home, and the Board of Trade hadn't ordered Andros to return to England.

The Archbishop of Canterbury entered the room and everyone stood. He stated, in a deep authoritative voice, "This hearing is called to order. We ask God's Grace in finding justice by this panel of judges." The archbishop then sat.

Everyone in the room took their seats, except for William Byrd II. Byrd, now twenty-three, had only once before made an appearance in a court of law. His energy and enthusiasm kept him standing.

Andros had appointed Byrd agent for the colony of Virginia in London. Byrd now served as Virginia's representative to the Board of Trade and to the Parliament. Byrd also understood the tobacco business and the main sources of wealth for the members of the Board of Trade. Though young, he was bright, well-educated, and very confident.

Byrd remained standing in a comfortable position and casually asked, in his slight Virginia drawl, "Would Reverend Blair please state his accusations, so they can be answered in an orderly fashion?"

Archbishop Tenison, a man of over sixty, was attired in the flowing, white silk blouse and tunic of an archbishop. "Young sir, please sit down. This hearing will be conducted under normal and regular procedures. We will begin by reviewing Reverend Blair's written charges." Tenison never looked at the other two hearing judges in making this decision.

Byrd refused to sit. He shouted to the panel of judges, "Reverend Blair has filled his church in Virginia with Scotchmen and is trying to make a national faction by the name of the Scottish party."

Henry Compton grew red in the face and shook his head. He responded. "There are not enough English priests who would go to the colonies. Needy clerics who've fled Scotland are available. It makes no difference to the church that they came from Scotland. They serve the church honestly wherever they were born."

Byrd shifted his weight and stood erect. He took a step forward toward the judges' bench and said, clearly and loudly, though still in his soft Virginia drawl, "Reverend Blair is here for himself, not for the Church or for Virginia or for the college. He's squandered payments to high-placed people in London that should have gone to the building of the college. He took the salary as president of the college even before the college was built. This conflicts with the college charter. Even yet there is no real college. It is a small grammar school, an Indian school, and almost no college faculty."

Tenison interrupted. "But this is the reason for this hearing. Reverend Blair has stated in writing that we must meet because he needs more money for the college."

Byrd was unimpressed. He had seen many great houses in more than one country, and Lambeth Palace wasn't the most impressive. His family's wealth rivaled that of any of the aristocratic families in Europe. He was used to being treated with respect due to his knowledge and wealth, and couldn't understand the treatment he was getting from the archbishop. He stood erect, then took another step toward the judges' bench and replied, "Please, Archbishop. Just read the college charter. We have a copy here for your perusal."

Tenison took a long look at this young man from Virginia. The archbishop had never seen the likes of this young, brash, confident youth. He didn't know how to deal with the upstart. Besides, he wasn't even English. Why would a royal governor choose a colonial boy to represent him in a high English ecclesiastical court? The archbishop felt insulted. Without consulting the other two judges, he said, "There is no time for the reading of documents. Please, Reverend Blair, begin your submission."

Blair spoke for more than an hour, reciting his work and his sacrifices. When he finally finished, Tenison said, "If I'd done all that, I'd probably take the salary of president as well."

Povey looked directly at Tenison when he said this, and then he leaned back to look at the ceiling. The archbishop then said, "Continue, Reverend Blair."

Blair then began his attack on Andros. "He was from the first an opponent of the clergy and the college. He caused me to be removed from his council, though the Commissary of the Church always sits on the Governor's Council."

Povey, of the King's Privy Council, interrupted. "But, Reverend Blair, you weren't ordered from the council by the Governor. You were suspended from the council because you hadn't been born in England. You were ordered from the council by council members following the law."

Blair shouted, in an angry voice, after strutting toward Povey, "Andros wanted me off the council, so I would not see the wasteful accounts of the colony."

Byrd jumped up at that. "Sirs, this is foolish, unsupported monologue. Can we have a true hearing on the facts?"

Tenison glared at Byrd. "Please sit down and keep silent." Compton smiled and said, "Well said, my Lord Archbishop!"

Blair continued a tirade against Andros that lasted another two hours. When Blair finished, Byrd asked, "May I now speak?"

Tenison replied, "What more is there to say? We've heard and read the full facts and need nothing more."

Compton again said, "Well said, my Lord Archbishop!" Povey said nothing.

Archbishop Tenison and the two other judges conferred

briefly with Povey doing most of the talking. The churchmen had great respect for this representative of the King's own council.

Finally Tenison announced the decision of the judges. "We find that many of Reverend Blair's complaints are well taken."

Blair was flustered. He stood and looked at the three judges, but couldn't make out the meaning of this decision. He asked, "But what next? Will you make any orders or do anything?"

Archbishop Tenison looked at Blair and said quietly, "This is an ecclesiastical court, and we find your moves on behalf of a college will likely favor the church in the future. If you want actions against a sitting governor you must deal with the Board of Trade. Why don't you write to John Locke?"

Blair who'd already met with Locke, and was here at Lambeth at Locke's suggestion, said nothing. When he returned to his rooms he wrote to Locke, asking him to present to the Board of Trade Blair's depictions of abuses and errors by Governor Andros. Locke never responded to Blair's letter. Instead, in March 1698, Governor Andros sent a letter to the Board of Trade asking to resign and return to England. Andros' letter cited his poor health, and the work he'd done for the colony in seeing to its defenses, fulfilling the king's mission during King William's War, and revising the laws.

The Board accepted Andros' resignation and drafted instructions for the next governor. They refused to reappoint Blair to the Governor's Council, but appointed Francis Nicholson as the new Governor of Virginia. They reasoned that even though they were a majority of Whigs, and Nicholson a Tory, Nicholson already had served as Lieutenant Governor of Virginia. They knew he badly wanted the job, and they had nobody else who was better qualified. Blair believed his lobbying helped Nicholson get the appointment, and he expected Nicholson to pay Blair for his services. In that, Blair would be sorely disappointed. Nicholson thought he got the job because he earned it.

Blair returned to Virginia in 1698 for Andros' last year in office. On October 21, 1698, six weeks before Nicholson was to take office, the state house in Jamestown burned. Nicholson, who loved to build things, now was determined to build a new capital city. He'd call it Williamsburg, after King William, and he'd personally lay out the plans for the streets.

GENEALOGY

SIR EDMUND ANDROS

With his service in Virginia finally over, Andros returned to England happily, and anticipated taking his place as the Bailiff of Guernsey. He had many friends and relatives who welcomed him back.

His good friend, John Churchill, had taken Daniel Parke as his aide-de-camp, and William Byrd II was back in London representing Virginia to the Parliament and the Board of Trade. Both of these young men and Andros' stepson Christopher Clapham occasionally visited Andros. He acted the part of an elderly uncle and enjoyed their company.

Andros was reasonably well off, but wasn't a wealthy man. He'd never used his position as Governor to amass property, as many other colonial governors had before him. In the past, royal governors had to be bribed to go to Virginia. Once there, they amassed as much property as was available.

Andros frowned upon land-grabbers and absentee landlords.

He didn't allow much of it in Virginia and he wasn't going to allow it in Guernsey. He took an interest in rebuilding the main manor house, and personally oversaw the planting of his gardens and farmland.

He spent most of his time in London, where he and his wife Elizabeth kept a town house. There, they heard the latest in court gossip and visited with friends. Andros knew many people at court, but didn't involve himself with politics. He supported his sovereign, King William, and was a Tory, but was pleased to be away from the rough-and-tumble of political maneuvering. His wife Elizabeth was pleased to be back as well.

Not long after his return to England, in 1702, King William died and was succeeded by Queen Anne. The succession of the monarchy in England remained a hot political issue. The ousted King James II still lived in France. He was Catholic, and Parliament decreed that England would permit only Protestant monarchs in the future.

Queen Anne was Protestant, married to Prince George of Denmark. She'd had four miscarriages and four children, but her first two daughters died before reaching the age of two; two other children, a son and a daughter, died soon after being born. Only the Duke of Gloucester remained, and in July 1700 he died at the age of eleven. The only Stuart remaining alive other than Anne was King James II, Anne's father.

Parliament responded by passing the Act of Settlement. After Anne, Princess Sophie of Hanover or her descendants now legally were next in line to the throne. This ensured a Protestant succession. Andros approved of the legislation. He well remembered being sent by King James II to Sweden to assess the possibility of James' marrying a Swedish princess.

Andros reminisced how different the world would have been had that succeeded. Instead, of course, James II had converted to Catholicism and married Mary of Modena. A Catholic king with Catholic heirs could have led to religious civil war again in England. Parliament had instead staged its "glorious revolution."

Andros was well acquainted with the new queen. John Churchill's wife, Sarah, was one of the queen's best friends. The Churchills had sided with the parliament and opposed King James in 1688, and persuaded Anne to support the accession of William of Orange. In 1702 in one of her first royal acts, Queen Anne granted Churchill the title of Duke of Marlborough. Anne's first ministers were Tories, and she favored them over the Whigs. Andros felt comfortable attending various ceremonial court functions.

In 1703 Andros mourned the death of his second wife, Elizabeth. They'd been married some fifteen years, and had weathered many storms together. Elizabeth had accompanied him to Virginia. Her son Christopher was like a son to Sir Edmund. Andros turned back to Guernsey for solace. In 1704 he was appointed Lieutenant Governor of Guernsey and saw to the island's defenses against threats from France.

That year, the allies faced France at the battle of Blenheim. The French threatened the city of Vienna and the rule of the Habsburg Emperor Leopold. John Churchill, now the Duke of Marlborough, commanded a large army in Germany and marched to the Danube where he joined forces with the armies of several small allies. The allies scored a decisive victory, and Marlborough sent his aide-de-camp, Daniel Parke, to relay the good news to the queen.

Queen Anne, overjoyed, complimented Parke and rewarded

him by appointing him Governor of the Leeward Islands. Finally Daniel Parke had achieved a title and authority of his own. He'd be rewarded with a governor's salary, the honor of a royally appointed office, and the joys of fame and celebrity. Byrd and Andros were proud of their good friend, as were the families in Virginia.

1704 was also a momentous year for William Byrd. His father died in Virginia, leaving vast estates and plantations. William returned to take over management of his new property. Two years later, he married Lucy Parke, Daniel Parke's daughter, who was then eighteen. The marriage was a double ceremony. That same day, May 4, 1706, Lucy's sister Frances, then twenty, married John Custis, stepson of Mrs. Tabitha Scarborough Smart Brown Custis Hill.

Edmund Andros, at the age of seventy in 1707, married his third wife, Elizabeth Fitzherbert. A new war with France raged, with many deaths reported to military families. He missed his young Virginia friends, but busied himself with the defense of Guernsey and social life in London. He prepared his last will and testament.

In it, he bequeathed money to train poor children to become apprentices. He also left money for his wife and stepson to live comfortably on and spread various sums to nephews, nieces and other family members.

The bulk of his estate he left to his nephew, John Andros. Sir Edmund's will ordered John to build a suitable house in Guernsey within two years of Sir Edmund's decease.

Andros died in 1714 at the age of seventy-six. Toward the end of his life, he saw the end of the war of the Spanish Succession, with the Treaty of Utrecht in 1713. Over the course of the war some 400,000 people were killed in Europe. Sir Edmund Andros, in his lifetime, had seen peace only in Virginia. He lived to see the Act of Union in 1707, which brought Scotland into the United Kingdom.

Andros was buried with honors with a marching retinue of sixty-six men, each carrying a white branch light. They were followed by twenty men on horseback, and six mourning coaches, each pulled by six horses. He was buried at St. Anne's Church in Soho, a building later destroyed by the Nazi blitz of London.

Though no traces remain of Sir Edmund's gravesite, his relatives remembered him with honor. Various descendants of the Andros family settled in Delaware and New Jersey, many changing their name to Andrews. A good number of them became Quakers. Thomas Andros of Guernsey wrote a memoir of Sir Edmund, published in 1853, and compiled *The Andros Tracts*, a description of Sir Edmund's accomplishments and activities, especially when Governor of the Dominion of New England.

The same year Sir Edmund died, Queen Anne also passed away, as did Princess Sophie of Hanover. The Stuart line ended when George I of Hanover, the son of Princess Sophie, became king of England. George I spoke little English and was an inactive monarch. He presided over a government that gradually evolved into a parliamentary system led by a prime minister. The following year, 1715, King Louis XIV of France also died.

FRANCIS NICHOLSON

Francis Nicholson is remembered for laying out the streets of Williamsburg, the colonial capital of Virginia which replaced Jamestown in 1699. He's remembered for naming two of the major streets after himself—Francis Street and Nicholson Street are two of Williamsburg's three main thoroughfares.

Nicholson died a bachelor in London in 1728. After becoming Governor of Virginia in 1698, he fought bitterly with James Blair. Blair again went to London to lobby against Nicholson with a Whig-dominated Board of Trade. In 1705 the Board of Trade recalled Nicholson, who rejoined the military to fight the French in Queen Anne's War.

Queen Anne's War followed the War of the Spanish Succession in North America. In 1710 the English lost Nova Scotia to the French, and Nicholson led an expedition that year that recaptured Port Royal, Nova Scotia. He returned to London with five Iroquois chiefs and petitioned the queen to allow him to join an expedition to conquer New France. When the naval part of the expedition failed, Nicholson called off the land expedition. He was then appointed Governor of Nova Scotia, where he remained till 1717.

He returned to London and was knighted in 1720. In his last royal appointment, Nicholson served as Royal Governor of South Carolina where he remained until he returned to England in 1725. In South Carolina, Nicholson beefed up the colony's defenses against the Indians. He also interested himself in building projects and education, and established new schools in the colony at his own expense. He's regarded by historians as one of South Carolina's finest colonial governors.

DANIEL PARKE

Daniel Parke, Governor of the Leeward Islands, died in 1710

in a riot caused by his own maladministration. His assassination surprised nobody in Virginia. In his last will and testament, he left his worldly goods to Lucy Chester, the illegitimate daughter of Katherine Chester. After her, he listed as an heir Julius Caesar Parke. He remembered his two daughters in Virginia, stating that if they should live, he left property to their sons and heirs provided they call themselves Parke. He left a thousand pounds each to Lucy and Frances, fifty pounds to Julius Caesar and nothing to his legal wife, Jane Ludwell Parke, who lived until 1746.

Daniel Parke left Jane saddled with substantial debts. His daughter Frances, also known as Fidelia, married John Custis and had five children. Frances' oldest son, Daniel Parke Custis, married Martha Dandridge and fathered four children, two of whom died in infancy. After the death of her first husband, Daniel Parke Custis, Martha Dandridge Custis married Colonel George Washington. Martha Washington was the first First Lady of the United States.

Lucy Parke Byrd, Daniel Parke's younger legitimate daughter, and William Byrd II had six children, three of whom died in infancy. William Byrd II accepted his father-in-law's debts as his own, a burden later inherited by his son William Byrd III. William Byrd III sold off a great deal of the Byrd property to pay these debts.

Both Lucy and William II were literary figures, and left detailed diaries describing life in the early eighteenth century. William was a surveyor, responsible for establishing the boundaries between Virginia and North Carolina. He published several diaries. The Byrd family of Virginia produced leading Virginian politicians up through the twentieth century.

WILLIAM ROSCOE

William Roscoe died in 1700 of unknown causes. He died leaving a relatively large tobacco plantation and one merchant ship to his heirs. At the time of his death, he had four sons and one daughter. He never counted Benjamin Harrison IV, the child he fathered with Sarah, as his son.

SARAH HARRISON BLAIR

Sarah Harrison Blair died in 1713 at the age of forty-three. She remains a general mystery, though several historians tell the story of her saying "no obey "at her wedding to Blair. Some works describe her as a half-wit, others as a foolish girl. She undoubtedly could read and write, and her marriage contract to William Roscoe is often quoted. William Byrd's diary records that she took to liquor later in her life, after William Roscoe's death.

The Harrison family, one of the wealthiest in Virginia, became leaders in support of revolution. Benjamin Harrison III, Sarah's brother, served as attorney general of the colony and Speaker of the House of Burgesses, but died at the age of thirty-three in 1710. He bought the patent for land on the James, and moved his family estate from Surry to the Berkeley Plantation. His son, Benjamin Harrison IV, expanded the family's land holdings considerably. He built a famous plantation house, installed large dock facilities, and became one of the largest tobacco planters in Virginia. He owned a fleet of merchant ships. Benjamin Harrison IV fathered ten children, the oldest being Benjamin Harrison V.

Benjamin Harrison V attended William and Mary, where he studied under law professor George Wythe, and was a classmate of Thomas Jefferson. While he was a student, the Harrison manor house was struck by lightning, killing his father and two sisters. Benjamin Harrison V left college and returned home to run the estates. He eventually became active in politics, and was elected to the House of Burgesses in 1764. In 1773 he was appointed delegate of Virginia to the Continental Congress in Philadelphia, and in 1776 was a Virginia signer of the Declaration of Independence.

Benjamin Harrison V served as Governor of Virginia in 1782. His son, William Henry Harrison, was Governor of Indiana Territory from 1801-1812, and was elected as the ninth President of the United States in 1840.

Benjamin Harrison VII, grandson of William Henry Harrison, was a senator from Indiana (1881-1887) and elected as the twenty-third President of the United States in 1888.

JAMES BLAIR

James Blair had no natural descendants. A clergyman and lobbyist, he amassed some personal wealth, but was disliked for most of his life by most of the people who knew him. His brother, Archibald Blair, became a leading merchant, a burgess, and was widely respected in the community. Archibald Blair had at least five children. One of Archibald's daughters, Elizabeth, married John Bolling, Jr., a great-grandson of Pocahontas and John Rolfe.

Probably the most lasting legacy of James Blair is the College of William and Mary. Blair was the first president of the college and remained in that office for fifty years. For the first thirty years, the college remained primarily a grammar school.

While Blair wished to produce ministers for the Church of

England, he was too avaricious to pay his faculty. Blair spent a lifetime fighting with governors, William and Mary faculty, and the Anglican ministers in Virginia. He managed to have a President's House built on the campus, but it wasn't completed until 1723.

After Blair's death in 1743, the college underwent a transformation. It housed a full faculty that taught the leading subjects of the day: natural science and mathematics, law, and moral philosophy. In 1747 the capitol building burned, and the burgesses moved to the college buildings. During this period, the college became a distinguished law school under the guidance of George Wythe, law professor to Thomas Jefferson and Benjamin Harrison V. George Washington obtained his license to be a surveyor from William and Mary in 1747.

William and Mary trained very few ministers of religion. Its most famous graduates were statesmen: Presidents Thomas Jefferson, James Monroe, and John Tyler, Chief Justice John Marshall, Speaker of the House Henry Clay, and sixteen signers of the Declaration of Independence. Phi Beta Kappa, the academic honor society, was founded at William and Mary in 1776.

In his final years, Blair remained avaricious as ever, amassing property wherever possible. He also continued to whine and complain about all governors. Governor William Gooch described Blair as "a vile old fellow, hated abominably by all men."

Blair became acting Governor for Gooch for eight months in 1740. Gooch had grave concerns, but Virginia was fortunate: no Indians or pirates threatened the colony and Blair never called the House of Burgesses into session. Blair, though sick and old, continued as Commissary and member of the Governor's Council till his death.

When he died at the age of 88, he left an estate five times the size of Edmund Andros's. He left property, slaves, and over a hundred acres to a nephew, the son of Archibald Blair. He was buried beside his wife in Jamestown and wrote his own epitaph:

Here lies buried
The Reverend and Honorable
James Blair A.M.
Born in Scotland,
Educated in the University of Edinburgh,
He came
First to England, then to Virginia;
In which part of the world
He filled the offices
For 58 years of Preacher of the Gospel,
For 54 of Commissary,
Of President of William and Mary,
Of a Councillor
to the British Governors,
Of President of the Council,
Of Governor of the Colony.
The comeliness of a handsome face
adorned him.
He entertained elegantly, in a cheerful, hospitable manner,
without luxury;
most munificently
he bestowed charity upon all needy persons;
in affability

he excelled.

For the College a well varied Library

he had founded.

Dying, his own Library

by will he bequeathed

for the purpose of informing students in Theology

and instructing the poorer youth.

He departed this life the XIV day before the Calends of May

MDCCXLIII

At the age of LXXXVIII.

Works more lasting than marble

will commend to his nephews

The surpassing praise of a well beloved old man.

One of the numerous ghost stories of Williamsburg relates that in 1750, just seven years after the death of James Blair, a small sycamore tree began growing near the flat tombstone that covered the graves of Sarah and James Blair. The tree grew and eventually split the tomb in two, pushing Sarah's grave closer to her parents and family, while leaving James alone. The splitting of the tomb also damaged and nearly effaced Blair's epitaph.

ACKNOWLEDGMENTS

This work is the result of several years of research which began when I became a docent in the gallery at Jamestown Settlement, a living history historical park located near the archeological site of the original Jamestown fort. The questions and comments of many visitors spurred my inquiries, and after a year I'd created a "Docent's Guide" of nearly a hundred typewritten pages. I'd also attended numerous lectures on related subjects provided by the educators at Jamestown Settlement.

The book is thus the product not only of my imagination, but of numerous published works, lectures, and comments by people with a knowledge and interest in American colonial history. I would like to thank them for their assistance and interest in this work.

First, I would l would like to acknowledge the artwork on the cover of this book. The illustration is the property of the National Park Service; the artist is Keith Rocco. A full-size copy of the painting can be seen in the lobby of the Visitor Center at Historic Jamestown, the site of the historic fort.

I would also like to thank my granddaughter, Catherine McLennan, for suggesting names of fictional characters. I'd also like to thank my other grandchildren, Sean McLennan, Heather Ashley, Cameron Ashley and Rachel Ashley, for humoring me and letting me know that they approve of and enjoy books.

In addition to the work at Jamestown Settlement, I conducted some research into original documents. Letters in the handwriting of James Blair and Francis Nicholson were found in the archives of the Earl Gregg Swem Library at the College of William and Mary. Some additional original documents also were found at the Rockefeller Library at Colonial Williamsburg. I managed to obtain published copies of Blair's report on *The Present State of Virginia and the College* and of the *Andros Tracts*, including a copy of Andros' Last Will and Testament. Blair's will disappeared in one of the Jamestown state house fires.

Information relating to legislative and legal matters was provided by the Library of Virginia, an institution operated by the state of Virginia. Other materials were found in numerous articles published in *Virginia Magazine*, the quarterly journal of the Virginia Historical Society.

Though many original documents have disappeared, some information was obtained from secondary sources. These include Warren Billings's *The Old Dominion in the Seventeenth Century,* a documentary history of Virginia, 1606-1700, and Billings's *A Little Parliament,* describing Virginia's General Assembly in the seventeenth century. A. J. Mapp, Jr.'s *The Virginia Experiment* discusses Virginia's role in the making of

America, 1607-1781. W. Kale's *Hark Upon the Gale* provides an illustrated history of the College of William and Mary. Mary Lou Lustig's *The Imperial Executive in America,* provides a detailed analysis of the career of Sir Edmund Andros. Parke Rouse, Jr.'s *James Blair of Virginia* provides a detailed biography of James Blair. Finally, L. B. Taylor, Jr. adds some color with his *The Ghosts of Williamsburg and Nearby Environs.*

CPSIA information can be obtained at www.ICGtesting.com
Printed in the USA
LVOW08s1350080716

495635LV00003B/43/P

9 781938 467615